The
Illustrated
Mum

Also by Jacqueline Wilson

The Suitcase Kid
Double Act
The Lottie Project
Bad Girls
The Story of Tracy Beaker
Vicky Angel
The Worry Web Site

For older readers
Girls in Love
Girls Under Pressure
Girls Out Late
Girls in Tears

The Illustrated Mum

Jacqueline Wilson

Delacorte Press

For Gina and Murray
and
Caroline and Georgina

Published by
Delacorte Press
an imprint of
Random House Children's Books
a division of Random House, Inc.
New York

Text copyright © 1999 by Jacqueline Wilson
Jacket illustration copyright © 2005 by Linda Davick
First American Edition 2005
First published in Great Britain by Doubleday,
a division of the Random House Group Ltd, in 1999

Visit us on the Web! www.randomhouse.com/kids
Educators and librarians, for a variety of teaching tools, visit us at
www.randomhouse.com/teachers

Library of Congress Cataloging-in-Publication Data

Wilson, Jacqueline.
The illustrated mum / Jacqueline Wilson.
p. cm.
Summary: Ten-year-old Dolphin is determined to stay with her family, no matter what,
but when her sister goes to live with her newly discovered father, sending their mother
further into manic depression, Dolphin's life takes a turn for the better.
ISBN 0-385-73237-6 (trade) — ISBN 0-385-90263-8 (GLB)
[1. Mothers and daughters—Fiction. 2. Manic-depressive illness—Fiction. 3. Sisters—
Fiction. 4. Single-parent families—Fiction. 5. Tattooing—Fiction. 6. England—Fiction.]
I. Title
PZ7.W6957Il 2005   [Fic]—dc22   2003070123

The text of this book is set in 11.5-point Palatino.

Printed in the United States of America

February 2005

10 9 8 7 6 5 4 3 2 1

BVG

CROSS

Marigold started going weird again on her birthday. Star remembered that birthdays were often bad times so we'd tried really hard. Star made her a beautiful big card cut into the shape of a marigold. She used up all the ink in the orange felt-tip coloring it in. Then she did two sparkly silver threes with her special glitter pen and added "Happy Birthday" in her best italic writing. They do calligraphy in Year Eight and she's very good at it.

I'm still in elementary school and I'm useless at any kind of writing so I just drew on my card. As it was Marigold's thirty-third birthday I decided I'd draw her thirty-three most favorite things. I drew Micky (I'd never seen him but Marigold had described him enough times) and Star and me. Then I drew the

Rainbow Tattoo Studio and the Victoria Arms and the Nightbirds club. I did them in the middle all clumped together and then round the edges I drew London and the seaside and the stars at night. My piece of paper was getting seriously crowded by this time but I managed to cram in a CD player with lots of Emerald City CDs and some high heels and a bikini and jeans and different-colored tight tops and lots of rings and bangles and earrings.

I was getting a bit stuck for ideas by this time and I'd rubbed out so often that the page was getting furry so I gave up and colored it in. I wanted to do a pattern of marigolds as a border but Star had used up the orange already, so I turned the marigolds into roses and colored them crimson. Red roses signify love. Marigold was very into symbols so I hoped she'd understand.

We gave her presents too. Star found a remixed version of Emerald City's greatest hits for only $2 at the Saturday morning market. I bought her a sparkly hair clasp, green to match her eyes. We even bought a special sheet of green tissue paper and a green satin ribbon to wrap up the presents.

"Do you think she'll like them?" I asked Star.

"You bet," said Star. She took the hair clasp and opened it up so its plastic claws looked like teeth. "I am a *great* present," she made it say, and then it bit the tip of my nose.

Marigold gave us both big hugs and said we were darlings but her great green eyes filled with tears.

"So why are you crying?" I said.

"She's crying because she's happy," said Star. "Aren't you, Marigold?"

"Mm," said Marigold. She sniffed hard and wiped her eyes with the back of her hand. She was shaking but she managed a smile. "There. I've stopped crying now, Dol, OK?"

It wasn't OK. She cried on and off all day. She cried when she listened to the Emerald City CD because she said it reminded her of old times. She cried when I combed her hair out specially and twisted it up into a chic plait with her new green clasp.

"God, look at my neck! It's getting all wrinkly," she said. She touched the taut white skin worriedly while we did our best to reassure her. "I look so *old.*"

"You're not old at all. You're young," said Star.

"Thirty-three," Marigold said gloomily. "I wish you hadn't written that right slap bang in the middle of your card, darling. I can't believe thirty-three. That was the age Jesus was when he died, did you know that?"

Marigold knew lots about the Bible because she was once in a church home.

"Thirty-three," she kept murmuring. "He tried so hard too. He liked kids, he liked bad women, he stuck up for all the alternative people. He'd have been so

3

cool. And what did they do? They stuck him up on a cross and tortured him to death."

"Marigold," Star said sharply. "Look at Dol's card."

"Oh yes, darling, it's lovely," Marigold said. She blinked at it. "What's it meant to be?"

"Oh, it's stupid. It's all a mess," I said.

"It's all the things you like most," said Star.

"That's beautiful," said Marigold, looking and looking at it. Then she started crying again.

"Marigold!"

"I'm sorry. It's just it makes me feel so awful. Look at the pub and the high heels and the sexy tops. These aren't mumsie things. Dol should have drawn . . . I don't know, a kitten and a pretty frock and . . . and Marks & Spencer. That's what mums like."

"It's not what you like and you're my mum," I said.

"Dol spent ages making you that card," said Star. She was starting to get red in the face.

"I know, I know. It's lovely. I *said*. *I'm* the hopeless case. Don't you get what I'm saying?" Marigold sniffed again. "Anyway, let's have breakfast. Hey, can I have my cake now? Birthday cake for breakfast! Great idea, eh, girls?"

We stared at her.

"We didn't get you a cake," said Star. "You *know* we didn't. We asked and you said a cake was the very last thing you wanted, remember?"

"No," said Marigold, looking blank.

She'd gone on and on that we mustn't get her a cake because she was sure she was starting to put on weight and the icing would only give her toothache and anyway she didn't even *like* birthday cake.

"I love birthday cake," said Marigold. "I always have a special birthday cake. You know how much it means to me because I never had my own special birthday cake when I was a kid. Or a proper party. I hate it that you girls don't want proper parties and you just go to stupid places like Laser Quest and McDonald's."

"They're not stupid," I said. Star got asked to lots of stuff but I'd never been to a McDonald's party and no one had ever asked me to a Laser Quest either. I hoped I'd maybe make lots of friends when I went to the high school. I wasn't in with the party crowd in my class. Not that I wanted to go to any of their parties. I wouldn't have been friends with any of that lot if you'd paid me. Except maybe Tasha.

"OK, OK, I'll go and get you a birthday cake," said Star. "Marks and Sparks opens early on a Saturday. You wait."

She took the housekeeping purse and rushed out, slamming the door.

"She's cross with me," said Marigold.

"No, she's not. She's going to get you your cake," I said.

"Cross cross cross," Marigold muttered, frowning.

"That's what they used to say in the home. 'I'm very cross with you, Marigold.' This old bat would bring her face right up close to me so that her eyes got so near they crossed too. 'Cross cross cross,' she'd say, and her spit would spray on my face. She was so mean, that one. She never hit us, she knew she wasn't allowed, but you could tell she really, really wanted to. She just *said* stuff. Cross cross cross."

"Marigold." I didn't know what else to say. I always got a bit scared when she talked like that, muttering fast, playing around with words. I wished Star would hurry back.

"Just words. Cross words!"

I giggled in case Marigold meant it to be a joke. She looked startled.

"We have crosswords at school," I said quickly. "I can't do them. I'm hopeless at spelling and stuff like that."

"Me too," said Marigold. "I hated school. I was always in trouble."

"Yep. Same here," I said, hoping that Marigold was better now. I was starving hungry. I took a handful of dry cornflakes to keep me going. Marigold helped herself too.

"Yet Star's clever," I said. "And she's got even cleverer since she went to the high school. A real old brainy-box."

"Well. She obviously takes after her father," said

Marigold. "Micky was the cleverest guy I ever met. So creative and artistic and yet sharp too. You couldn't ever fool him."

"I wish he was my dad too," I said.

Marigold patted me sympathetically.

"Never mind. I've got you for my mum." I said it to make her happy but it started her off crying again.

"What kind of a useless stupid mum am I?" she said.

"You're the best ever mum. Please don't cry again. You'll make your eyes go all red."

"Red eyes, ropey neck, maudlin mood. What a mess! What have I got to show for my thirty-three years, eh? Apart from you two lovely girls. What would Micky make of me if he came back now? He always said I had such potential and yet I haven't done anything."

"You do lots and lots of things. You paint and you make beautiful clothes and you dance and you work at the studio and—and—"

"If I don't do something with my life soon I never will. I'm getting old so quickly. If only Micky would come back. I was a different person when I was with him. He made me feel so . . ." She waved her thin arms in the air, her bangles jangling. "Can't find the words. Come here, Dol."

She pulled me close for a cuddle. I nestled against her, breathing in her magical musky smell. Her silky red hair tickled me. I stroked it, letting it fan out through my fingers.

"Your roots need doing soon. And you've got a few split ends. I'll snip them off for you, if you like."

"You still going to be a hairdresser, Dol?"

"You bet," I said, turning my fingers into scissors and pretending to chop.

"I remember when you cut all the hair off your Barbie doll," said Marigold.

"And Star's too. She was so mad at me."

"You girls. I wish I'd had a sister."

"Well. You're like our big sister."

"I feel like I'm at a crossroads in my life, Dol. Cross. Hey, you know what? How about if I got a cross for a tattoo?"

"You haven't got much space left," I said, rubbing her decorated arms.

Marigold was examining herself, peering this way and that.

"How about right here, across my elbow? Brilliant! The cross could go up and down my arm. I need a bit of paper." She used the back of my birthday card but I didn't really mind. She sketched rapidly, her teeth nipping her lower lip as she concentrated. I peered over her shoulder.

"You're so good at drawing," I said wistfully.

Her hand was still shaking but the pen line was

smooth and flowing as she drew an elegant long Celtic cross with roses and ivy twining round it.

"Roses," she said, looking up at me. "Like the ones on your card, Dol."

I felt immensely proud. But also worried. I knew what Star was going to say.

"It's a lovely picture," I said. "Couldn't you just keep it a picture on paper? We could get a special frame for it and you could hang it over your bed."

"I want it to be a picture on *me*," said Marigold, her eyes glittering green. "I wonder if Steve's got any early appointments? I can't wait! I'll get him to trace it and do it now. Special birthday present." She leapt up. "Come on!"

"But Star's getting your birthday cake!"

"Oh!" She screwed up her face in disappointment. "Oh yes. Well, come *on*, Star. Where's she got to? Why did she have to go out now to get this cake?"

This was so unfair of Marigold I couldn't look her in the eyes. She was terrible when she twisted every-thing about. She always did it when she got worked up. I knew I should tell her she wasn't being fair to Star but I couldn't make myself. It was so special being Marigold and me.

Star was ages. Marigold paced the flat in her high heels, groaning theatrically and watching the clock. When Star came back at last, carefully carrying a plastic bag on upturned hands, Marigold had to make an extreme effort.

"Star! You've been such a long time, sweetie!"

"Sorry. There were heaps of people. And I had to walk back carefully because I didn't want the cake to get bashed. I do hope you like it. I didn't know whether to pick the fruit or the sponge. I got the sponge because it was cheaper—but maybe you like fruit more?"

"Whichever," said Marigold carelessly. "Come on then, let's have a slice of cake."

She was already pulling it out of the box, barely looking at it. She didn't even put it on a proper plate. She rummaged in the drawer for a sharp knife and went to cut the first slice.

"You've got to make a wish!" said Star.

Marigold raised her eyebrows but closed her eyes and wished. We didn't need to ask what she was wishing for. I saw her lips say the word "Micky." Then she was hacking away at the cake and gulping her slice so quickly she sprayed crumbs everywhere.

"What's the big hurry?" said Star.

I stopped eating my own slice of cake.

"I'm going to try to catch Steve early, before any clients. I've just designed the most amazing symbolic tattoo," said Marigold.

"No," said Star. "Not another. You *promised*."

"But this is so beautiful, darling. A cross because

I'm at the crossroads. Look!" Marigold waved her design.

"You've spoilt Dol's birthday card," said Star.

"No she hasn't," I said quickly.

"You said it was sick and pathetic getting yourself tattooed again and again. You said you'd save up for laser treatment to get them removed. You *said*," Star said, her voice rising.

"I said a whole load of stuff just to keep you happy, darling. But I love all my tattoos. They're all so special to me. They make *me* feel special."

"They make you look like a circus freak," said Star.

There was a sudden silence. We stood looking at each other in shock and embarrassment, hardly able to believe what Star had just said. Even Star seemed astonished.

"OK, so I'm a freak," said Marigold shakily. "I don't care. I don't have to conform to your narrow view of society, Star. I've always lived my life on the outside edge."

"Now you're sounding like some corny old film. Why can't you act *normal*?"

"I don't want to be normal," said Marigold. "I can't figure out why you do all of a sudden. What's the matter with you, Star?"

"Maybe I'm growing up. When are you going to grow up, Marigold?" She seized her slice of cake and crumpled it into tiny crumbs. Then she brushed her hands and ran into our bedroom.

Marigold and I looked at each other. Marigold tried to look like she didn't care. She put her hand to her head as if she was trying to hold it together.

"What should I do?" she whispered to me.

"Star didn't really mean it," I said. "She was just upset because she thought you didn't like the cake."

"I know she's got this thing about tattoos—but I *want* the cross, Dol."

I shrugged helplessly. Star was always the one who told Marigold what to do. I wasn't any good at it.

"It will look incredible, I just know it," said Marigold. "I have to go now or Steve won't have time. Will you come too?"

I hesitated. I wasn't like Star, who had refused to set foot in the Rainbow Tattoo Studio. I found it fascinating, though I was sometimes a bit scared of some of the customers. Steve himself was kind of scary too, with his shiny bald head and his long beard and his pointed tongue with a stud through the end. I hated seeing it flash silver in his mouth. He knew this and stuck his tongue out at me whenever he saw me.

"Please," Marigold pressed. "I'll need you. It'll hurt."

"You said it doesn't hurt much at all."

"It will hurt on the elbow. It's always painful on a joint."

"Then *why* . . . ?"

"It'll be more special if I have to suffer for it," said Marigold.

"That's silly," I said.

"I'll need you there so I can hold your hand to be brave," said Marigold. "If you don't come I might go really mad and get Steve to do the cross on my face. Up the forehead, down the nose, across both cheeks." She shook her head at me. "Oh, Dol, I'm *joking*."

I wasn't sure. When Marigold was in this sort of mood she could do the craziest thing on a sudden whim. Maybe she really did need me to go with her. I was worried but I also felt very grown-up and special. It was me she needed, not Star.

I still felt bad about Star, though.

"Come on, Dol," said Marigold, desperate to be off.

"Wait a second," I said, and went to our bedroom.

I hesitated and then knocked on the door in case Star was crying and didn't want me to see. She didn't answer. I timidly peeked round the door. She was sitting on the end of the bed, her fists clenched in her lap. Her face was hidden by her long hair.

"Star? Star, she wants me to go with her."

Star shrugged as if it was nothing to do with her.

"Maybe Steve will have an early customer," I said. "Then he won't be able to do it. Or maybe she'll change her mind again. You know what she's like."

"I know what she's like," Star said slowly. Her teeth were clenched too.

"Star?"

"Stop bleating my name like that, it's so *irritating*."

"Do you mind if I go with her? I'd better, hadn't I?"

"You do what you want."

"Can't you come too?"

Star looked at me witheringly. "I'm not going near that stupid place."

I waited, trying to think of some way to make everything better.

"It's a great birthday cake, Star."

I wasn't getting anywhere. I suddenly heard the front door bang. I had to leave Star. I ran hard after Marigold. She was halfway down the stairs.

"Wait for me!"

"I thought you maybe weren't coming," said Marigold. She laughed. "But you are, you are, you are!" She caught hold of me on the first-floor landing and swung me round.

"What a racket!" Mrs. Luft was down at the front door sorting through the post. She seemed to be addressing an invisible audience. "Do they have to be so noisy on the stairs? Up and down, late at night, first thing in the morning. Some people have no consideration."

"Any post for me?" Marigold asked. She always got extra hopeful on her birthdays and Christmas, just in case Micky decided to get in touch. Ever since we'd been given the Housing Trust flat she'd renewed the postal forwarding service every three months. It was the one thing she never forgot.

"Electricity bill," said Mrs. Luft, handing it over.

"Well, I don't think I'll bother with that," said Marigold, tossing the unopened bill onto the old table in the hallway.

I looked at it anxiously. Mrs. Luft sniffed.

"That's a very responsible attitude, I must say," she announced. "Some people take pride in paying their bills on time. Others are downright feckless. Spend, spend, spend—and lets the state fork out for her and her children."

Marigold told Mrs. Luft to go away and mind her own business. She didn't say it politely. She used short sharp words.

"Yes, that's just the sort of language I'd expect from *her*," said Mrs. Luft. She shuffled into her flat, her backless slippers slapping the floor at each step.

"Mad old bat," said Marigold, taking my hand. "Come on, let's see if we can run all the way."

She was faster than me at running even though she was wearing high heels. I hung back and had to stop and gasp for breath at every new street, a stitch in my side. It was still hurting when we got to the Rainbow Tattoo Studio. The Closed sign was on the door but when Marigold tapped the opaque glass with her long fingertips Steve came to the door.

"Uh-oh," he said, giving her one glance. "I'm not starting any long customized job now, Goldie. I've got a guy coming in at ten."

"Oh, Steve, be a honey. Which guy? If he's a biker he won't make it in till eleven at the earliest. And if he's a first-timer then it's odds on he won't even turn up. *Please*, sweetheart. It's my birthday. And it's just this *gorgeous* design. You'll love it. Look!"

She waved my card at him.

"Bit intricate, isn't it?" he said, looking at my birth-day drawing.

I blushed, not wanting him to laugh at me.

"Steve!" said Marigold impatiently.

"Nice drawing," Steve said to me. Then he turned the card over. "Ah."

"It's great, isn't it. I thought right here." Marigold tapped her left elbow.

Steve tutted, the silver flashing in his tongue.

"You're paying, I take it?"

"Out my wages," said Marigold.

"But we only need you here the odd day or so when someone needs a custom job."

"I'll come in and do flash work—whatever."

"I don't trust you to do flash work properly, Goldie. Remember that guy who wanted the samurai arm piece and you did the mouth all smiley instead of sneering?"

Marigold was smiling herself. She bent over to Steve and put her arms round his neck, whispering in his ear.

I turned my back on her and looked at the wall of flash. They had all the usual designs on display, most of them pretty boring stuff, dragons and tigers and skulls and basic Celtic designs. I could understand why Marigold got so sick of tracing out the same designs again and again. No wonder she sometimes gave the dragon flame-breath or the tiger a little cub or placed a perky little wig on top of the skull.

She was still wound round Steve. He soon weakened.

"OK, OK, I'll do your cross. Only no shrieking the place down. I don't want you frightening away any potential customers."

"I won't even whimper," she promised.

Steve tinkered with his needle bar, bunching the needles at various angles.

"You're a genius, Steve," Marigold said, tracing her cross design onto duplicating paper. "No one can ink like you."

"Flattering witch," he said, wiping her arm with alcohol and then spraying it with soap and water. He carefully stuck the duplicating paper down, rubbed it all over and then left the picture in place.

"You're sure, Goldie?"

"Surer than sure," she said, taking my hand with her free right arm.

Steve rubbed Vaseline over the design, poured out a capful of color, put on his rubber gloves and started the machine.

I couldn't look for a long time. I held Marigold's hand tight as tight, while her nails dug a deep groove in my palm. Her eyes were watering and she bit hard on her bottom lip, but she was as good as her word, not making a whimper.

The machine buzzed loudly. Steve whistled tunelessly through his teeth, his way of concentrating. He stopped every now and then and sprayed Marigold's arm and dabbed it dry.

I dared look. I saw the black line of the cross taking shape. It took well over an hour before it was finished. Two customers were kept waiting but Steve let them see what he was doing and they watched, fascinated.

"Right. Done!" Steve said at last.

Marigold got up very slowly, straightening her arm with extreme caution. The front of her shirt was damp with sweat. Her face was chalk white but when she saw the new cross tattoo in the mirror it flooded pink.

"Oh, Steve, it's going to look wonderful!"

"It's your design, babe," said Steve, coating it with special ointment.

He went to wrap it in a bandage but Marigold stepped aside.

"Let me look a minute more." She craned round to examine every detail.

"That's a truly cool tattoo," said one of the customers. "I reckon it would look great on my lady. Will you do a cross on her exactly like that?"

"I'll design her own personal cross, if that's what she'd like," said Marigold. "But this one's mine."

She let Steve put the bandage on and then grinned at me.

"This one's mine too," she said, ruffling my hair. "Come on, Dol. See you, Steve, darling."

He was busy breaking the used needles off the bar and putting the equipment in the sterilizer.

"Don't forget this," he said, pointing to my card.

"I don't need the design. It's permanent now," said Marigold, tossing it in the bin.

"It's on the back of your birthday card," Steve reminded her.

"Whoops!" said Marigold, retrieving the card. "Sorry, Dol."

"It's OK," I muttered.

"Hey, you're not going to go all sulky on me too, are you? It's my *birthday*. We're going to have *fun*," said Marigold.

It didn't really work. Star was barely speaking

when we got back. When she saw Marigold's bandage she screwed up her face in disgust.

We had the rest of the birthday cake for lunch. Marigold bought wine for herself and juice for Star and me.

"So we can all drink to the birthday girl," she said.

She drank her wine in less than half an hour and then said she felt a little sleepy. She curled up on the sofa, her arm carefully out to one side. She fell asleep in the middle of a sentence.

Star stared at her.

"She only drank so much because her arm hurts," I said.

"So whose fault is that?" said Star.

But with Marigold out of it Star was much better company. She'd done all her boring old weekend homework so now she was free to play with me.

"I wish we could watch television," I said.

The rental firm had taken our television and video recorder away the past week because Marigold hadn't kept up the payments. She promised she'd see about getting us a new set but she hadn't done anything about it yet.

"Will you *play* television, Star?" I begged.

"Oh, honestly, Dol, you and your dopey games," she groaned.

"Please?"

"Just for ten minutes then."

We went into our bedroom, shutting the door on the sleeping Marigold. Star wouldn't try properly at first, and said she felt stupid, but eventually she got into it too. I said we'd do *Top of the Pops* first because I knew Star liked being all the different singers. Then we did this children's hospital program and I was a little girl dying tragically of cancer and Star was my nurse giving me treatment. Then we played vets and Star's old teddy and my china dog and the troll doll we'd won at a fair were the pets in distress.

Star started to get bored with this, so I said we'd do some soaps because she's great at accents, so for a while we played *Neighbours* and then swopped to *East-Enders* and then Star herself suggested we do *Friends*. We both wanted to be Rachel and then we got onto hairstyles and we stopped the television game and played hairdressers instead.

Star played for ten times ten minutes and it was great. We almost forgot Marigold.

She woke up in a snappy mood, going on about the cross again, muttering to herself, holding her bandaged arm. She spent ages in the bedroom after tea.

"Are you all right, Marigold?" I called eventually, standing outside the door.

"I'm fine fine fine, never finer," said Marigold.

She came out all dressed up in her shortest skirt

and highest heels, her black chenille sweater hiding her bandage.

"You're going out," Star said flatly.

"Of course I'm going out, darling. I've got to celebrate my birthday," said Marigold.

Star sighed heavily.

"Don't be like that. I'm just nipping down to the Vic. I'll be back in a couple of hours, promise."

We both looked at her.

"I *promise*," she said again. She stroked her bulky arm gingerly. "I'm at the crossroads. I'm going to take the right turning now. You'll see. I'll be back by ten. Half ten at the latest."

We stayed up till midnight. Then we gave up and went to bed.

MARIGOLD

I woke up too early. It wasn't properly light yet. My heart started thudding.

I scrabbled around for my silk scarf. I always like to take it to bed with me. Star calls it my cuddle blanket. When she's being really mean to me she sometimes hides it.

I could only feel rumpled sheet and lumpy pillow. I wriggled up the bed a bit and then realized I was lying on my scarf. I rubbed it quick against my nose, snuffling in its sweet powdery smell.

I still felt frightened. Then I remembered.

"Star!" I leant out of my bed and reached for her. "Star, wake up. It's morning. Nearly. Do you think Marigold's come back?"

"Go and look," Star mumbled from under her covers.

I was scared to look. Scared in case she was in a state. Scared in case she had someone with her. Scared in case she hadn't come back at all.

"You look, Star," I begged. "You're the eldest."

"I'm sick of being the eldest. I'm sick of being the one who has to try hardest all the time. I'm sick sick sick of it," said Star. Her voice was thick. I thought she might be crying.

"OK, I'll look," I said, and I got out of bed.

My heart was like a little fist inside my chest, punching and punching.

"Don't be so stupid," I whispered in Star's voice. "She'll be back. She'll be in bed fast asleep. Just go and take one peep."

I crept across our room, over the landing. I stood in front of Marigold's open door. Had it been open or shut last night? I couldn't remember. I could see the edge of her bed but no mound under the cover, no foot poking out palely from beneath the sheet.

"She'll be curled up in a ball, legs tucked up. That's why you can't see her. She always sleeps like that. Go and *look*," I whispered.

I stood still for more than a minute. Then I whispered her name. Nothing. I stepped into her room. It was empty. I knew it was empty with one glance but I pulled the covers back, I lifted the pillow, as if she might be curled so small she could be hiding underneath. I looked under the bed and felt for her there with my hands. I rolled little dustballs in my fingertips, breathing very quickly, wondering what on earth to do next.

I looked in the bathroom and loo. I went into the kitchen to see if she could be there, my mind conjuring up a crazy image of Marigold making toast, hours early for breakfast. The kitchen was empty. The tap dripped, plink plink plink. None of us knew how to change the washer. I stood watching it, blinking in time until my eyes blurred.

I went back to Star. She was still under the covers but I could tell by her breathing that she was wide awake and listening.

"She's not back."

Star sat up. I heard her swallow. I could almost hear the buzz of her thoughts.

"Look in the loo," she said.

"I have. She's not anywhere."

"What's the time?"

"It's half past five."

"Oh," Star sounded frightened too now. "Well. Maybe . . . maybe she's not planning on getting back till breakfast."

"Star. What if . . . what if she doesn't come back?"

"She will."

"But what if something bad has happened to her?"

"*She's* the one who does bad things," said Star. She reached out and caught hold of me by the wrist. "Come on. She'll be all right. She's probably met some guy and she's with him."

"But she wouldn't stay out all night long," I said, scrabbling into her bed beside her.

"Well, she has, hasn't she? Hey, you're freezing."

"Sorry."

"Never mind. Here." Star pressed her warm tummy against my back and made a lap for me with her legs. Her arms went round me tight and hugged me.

"Oh, Star," I said, crying.

"Shhh. Don't get my pillow all wet and snotty."

"She *is* all right, isn't she?"

"She's all wrong wrong wrong. But she'll be back any minute now, you'll see. We'll go back to sleep and then we'll wake up and the first thing we'll hear is Marigold singing one of her stupid songs, right?"

"Yes. Right. I do like it when you're being nice to me."

"Well. It's no fun being nasty to you. It's like kicking Bambi. Let's try to sleep now."

"I love Bambi." I tried to think of all the best bits in *Bambi*. I thought of Bambi frolicking with Flower with all the birds twittering and Thumper singing away, tapping his paw. Then my brain flipped to fast forward.

"What?" said Star, feeling me stiffen.

"Bambi's mother gets killed."

"Oh, Dol. Shut up and go to *sleep*."

I couldn't sleep. Star couldn't either, though she pretended at first. We turned every ten minutes, fitting round each other like spoons. I tried counting to a hundred, telling myself that Marigold would be back by then. Two hundred. Three hundred.

I wanted my silk scarf but I'd left it in my bed. I put the end of the sheet over my nose instead and fingered the raised edge of the hem. It started to get lighter. I shut my eyes but in the dark inside my head there was a little television showing me all the things that might have happened to Marigold. It was so scary I poked the corner of the sheet in my eye. It hurt a lot but the television set didn't even flicker. I tried to hum so that I couldn't hear it. I banged my head on the pillow to see if I could switch it off that way.

"What on earth are you doing?" said Star.

"Just trying to get comfy."

"You're going about it in a funny way."

"It's to stop myself thinking stuff. It's so scary."

"Look. Let's tell each other really really scary stories. We'll think about that, right? There was this video I saw at that sleepover I went to, and there were these girls in a house, and they played these real witchy tricks on another girl, so that when she got out of bed she stepped into this great squirmy mass of spiders and slugs and snakes, and she screamed and starting running, and all these *other* snakes dropped on her head and writhed round her neck and down inside her clothes—"

"Shut up, shut up!" I said, shrieking—and yet it helped. We were suddenly just us playing a scary game and it was almost fun.

I hadn't ever seen any horror videos but I was quite good at making them up. Star told me this story about a dead man who comes back to kill all these kids and his fingers are like long knives so he can rip people in half.

"I've got a better ghost, a *real* one. Mr. Rowling!" I said triumphantly.

Mr. Rowling was the old man who lived upstairs. He had this illness when we first moved in here and he knew he was dying and he said he was going to leave his body to medical science. I'd had to ask Star what that meant and when she told me it had given me nightmares, thinking of medical students cutting up all these little bits of Mr. Rowling.

"Mr. Rowling couldn't be scary. He was quite a nice old man," said Star.

"Yes, he might have been nice when he was alive, but he's really really scary now, because those medical people cut out his eyes so he's just got horrible bleeding sockets and they've sawn off great strips of his skin and torn out his liver and his kidneys and left a big mess of intestines sticking out all smelly and slimey, and all the rest of him is rotting away so that when he walks around little moldery bits of him fall off like big dandruff. He wishes and wishes he hadn't left his body to medical science because it hurts so badly so every night he rises up off the dissecting table and he trails messily back to this house where he liked living and he's maybe upstairs right this minute. Yes, he is, and he's thinking, I like that Star, she was always nice to me, I'm going to go and see how she is, and he's coming, Star, he's slithering along, dripping maggots, getting nearer and nearer. . . ."

Something creaked and we both screamed. Then we sat up, ears straining, wondering if it was Marigold back at last. But then we heard the whoosh of the boiler in the kitchen. It was just the hot water system switching itself on.

"Oh well," said Star. "We could just go and have a bath in a minute."

"Let's have one more look round the flat. She could have crept in while we were cuddled up. We could have gone to sleep without realizing it," I said.

We both padded all over the flat though we knew there wasn't a chance Marigold was there. So then we went and had a bath together, because the water wasn't hot enough for two baths. It was like being little kids again. Star washed my hair for me and then I did hers. I'd always longed to look like Star but I especially envied her beautiful long fair hair. Mine was mouse and it was so fine it straggled once it grew down to my shoulders.

I suppose Star looked like her father and I looked like mine. Neither of us looked like Marigold, though we both had a hint of her green eyes.

"Witch's eyes," Marigold always said.

Star's eyes were bluey-green, mine more gray-green. Marigold's eyes were emerald, the deepest glittery green, the green of summer meadows and seaweed and secret pools. Sometimes Marigold's eyes glittered so wildly it was as if they were spinning in her head like Catherine wheels, giving off sparks.

"What if Marigold—" I started.

"Stop what-iffing," said Star. "Hey, I thought you fancied yourself as a hairdresser? I've still got heaps of soap in my hair." She tipped jugfuls of water over her head and then started toweling herself dry.

I watched her.

"Quit *staring*," Star snapped.

I couldn't help staring at her. It was so strange seeing her with a chest. I peered down at my own but it was still as flat as a boy's.

"Two pimples," said Star, sneering at me. "Turn round, let me do your back."

We got dressed in our school clothes. Well, our version of school clothes. I wore one of Marigold's dresses she'd cut small for me, black with silver moon and star embroidery. I called it my witch dress and thought it beautiful. It still smelt very faintly of Marigold's perfume. I sniffed it now.

"Is it sweaty?" said Star.

"No!"

"I don't know why you keep wearing that old thing anyway. You just get teased."

"I get teased anyway," I said.

Star used to wear much weirder outfits when she was at my school but nobody ever dared tease Star. She changed when she started at the high school. She wore the proper uniform. She *wanted* to. She got money off Marigold the minute she got it out the post office and went to the school's special uniform sale and got herself a hideous gray skirt and blazer and white blouses and even a tie.

She customized them when she went into Year Eight, shortening the skirt until it was way up above her knees, and she put pin badges all over the blazer lapels. It was the way all the wilder girls in her class altered their uniform. Star didn't seem to want to do it her way anymore.

She checked herself in the mirror and then fiddled with my dress.

"Sweaty or not, it needs a wash."

"No, it'll spoil it."

"It's spoilt already. And the hem's coming down at the back. Here, I'll find a pin."

She tucked the wavy hem neatly into place and then stood up.

"Right," she said. She glanced at the kitchen table, the bowls and spoons set out Three Bears style.

"I'm not hungry," I said.

"Me neither," said Star. "Tell you what. Marigold's got the purse, but I've got that pound I found down the park. We'll buy chocolate on the way to school, right?"

"Do we have to go to school?"

"Yes."

"But—"

"It'll be worse if we just stay here, waiting. We'll both go to school like normal. Only you won't tell anyone that she's gone missing, will you?"

"Has she really . . . gone missing?"

"I don't know. But if you start blabbing about it, or even go round all sad and snively so that some nosey teacher starts giving you the third degree then I'm telling you, Dol, they'll get the social workers in and we'll both end up in care."

"No!"

"Maybe not even together."

"Stop it."

"So keep your mouth shut and act like you haven't got a care in the world. Don't look like that. *Smile!*"

I tried. Star sighed and put her arm round me. "She'll probably be back right after we've left for school."

"We'd better leave her a note."

"What?" Star glared at me.

"In case she wonders if we're OK."

"Oh yes. Like she wondered if we were OK last night," said Star.

"She can't help the way she is."

"Yes she can," said Star, and she marched us both out of the flat.

I made out I needed to go to the toilet when we were down on the main landing, so Star gave me the key. I charged back up the stairs and in at our door and then I tore out a page from my project book and scribbled:

We are at schol.
Bak soon.
Hop your okay.
We are.
Lots and lots and
xtra lots of lov
form Dolly and Star.

Then I ran back downstairs again. Mrs. Luft came to the door in her dressing gown, her hair pinned into little silver snails all over her head.

"I've told you girls enough times! Stop charging up and down the stairs like that. My whole flat shakes. And the stairs won't stand it. There's the dry rot. I've spoken to the trust a dozen times but they don't do anything. You'll put your foot right through if you don't watch out."

I stood still, staring down at the old wooden stairs. I imagined them crumbling beneath me, my foot falling through, all of me tumbling down into the dark rotting world below. I edged downward on tiptoe, holding my breath.

"Come on, Dol, we'll be late," said Star. When I got nearer she whispered, "*She's* the one that's talking rot."

I sniggered. Mrs. Luft sniffed disapprovingly, folding her arms over her droopy old-lady chest.

"How's that mother of yours, then?" she asked.

I stood still again.

"She's fine," said Star.

"No more funny turns?" said Mrs. Luft unpleasantly.

"I don't know what you mean," said Star, and grabbed me. "Come *on*, Dol."

"Dol. Star," Mrs. Luft muttered mockingly, shaking her head.

"Old cow," Star said as we went out the house.

"Yes. Old cow," I said, imagining Mrs. Luft with horns springing out of her curlers and udders bunching up the front of her brushed nylon nightie.

Star went into the paper shop and bought us both a Mars bar. I sunk my teeth into the firm stickiness, taking big bites so that my mouth was overwhelmed with the taste of chocolate.

"I just love Mars bars," I said indistinctly.

"Me too," says Star. "Good idea, eh? Right, you come and wait for me outside school this afternoon, OK?"

"OK," I said. I did my best to smile. As if I didn't have a care in the world.

"You can have the rest of my Mars if you like," said Star, thrusting the last little piece of hers into my hand.

She ran off to join up with a whole gaggle of high school girls getting off the bus. I trudged on toward Holybrook Primary. Nearly everyone got taken by their mothers, even the kids in Year Six. Marigold hardly ever took me to school. Mostly she stayed in bed in the morning. I didn't mind. It was easier that way. I didn't like to think about the times when she *had* come to the school, when she'd gone right in and talked to the teachers.

I ran to stop myself thinking, and touched the school gate seven times for luck.

It didn't work. We had to divide up into partners for letterwriting and no one wanted to be my partner. I ended up with Ronnie Churley. He said, "Rats," and sat at the furthest edge of the seat, not looking at me. So I wrote a long letter to myself instead of doing the exercise properly and Miss Hill said I should learn to listen to instructions and gave me nought out of ten.

Ronnie Churley was furious with me because he got nought too. He said it wasn't fair, it was all my fault. He whispered he and his mates were going to get me at lunchtime.

I said, "Like I'm supposed to be *scared*?" in a very fierce bold Star voice.

Only I *was* scared of Ronnie Churley, and he had a lot of mates. I hid at lunchtime, lurking in the cloakrooms. I stood on a bench and looked out of the window at the playground. Ronnie Churley and his gang were picking on Owly Morris instead of me. I felt a bit mean about poor Owly but I couldn't help it. I wandered round the cloakroom looking at everybody's boring jackets and coats and working out how Marigold would make them look pretty—a velvet trim here, a purple satin lining, little studs in a Celtic design, an embroidered green dragon breathing crimson fire—when Mrs. Dunstan, the deputy head, walked past with some little kid who'd fallen over in the playground. I dropped the sleeve of someone's coat like it was red hot.

Mrs. Dunstan asked what I was doing and didn't I know children weren't allowed in the cloakrooms at playtimes? I got pink in the face because I hate being told off. Mrs. Dunstan frowned at me.

"Why were you touching that coat, hmm?"

My pink became peony.

"You weren't going through the pockets, were you?"

I stood rooted to the spot, staring at her.

"I'm not a thief!" I said.

"I didn't say you were," said Mrs. Dunstan. "Well, run along now, and don't let me catch you here again."

I nearly ran right out of the school and all the way home. But it would be even worse there by myself. I had to wait to meet Star that afternoon.

I remembered my promise. I put my head up high, stretched my lips and sauntered off as if I didn't have a care in the world. I could feel Mrs. Dunstan's gaze scorching my back.

I got to the playground thirty seconds before the bell. Thirty seconds can seem a lifetime when Ronnie Churley and his mates are punching you in the stomach and giving you Chinese burns on each wrist.

I couldn't think straight during the afternoon. I just kept thinking about the flat and whether Marigold was in it. I inked a careful picture of her marigold tattoo with its full head and pointed leaves and swirly stem, chewing hard on the tip of my pen. I drew another Marigold and another. I bent my head and whispered her name over and over again. I started to convince myself it was the only way to make her safe.

"Who's she talking to?"

"Talking to herself!"

"She's a nutter."

"Just like her mum."

I turned round to Kayleigh Richards and Yvonne Mason and spat at them. The spit landed on Kayleigh's math book. My mouth was inky so it made a little blue pool on the page.

She screamed.

"Yuck! She spat on my book! It nearly landed on me. I could catch a terrible disease off of her. She's *disgusting.*"

Miss Hill told Kayleigh to calm down and stop being so melodramatic. She mopped up the spit herself with blotting paper and then stood over me.

"What is the *matter* with you today?"

I clenched my fists and put my chin up and smiled as if I didn't have a care in the world.

I was sent to stand outside the classroom for insolence. Then when the bell went Miss Hill gave me this long lecture, going on and on, and I had to get right over to the high school to meet Star. If I wasn't there when she got out she'd maybe think I'd gone home already. Then *she'd* go off without me.

"You're not even listening to me!" said Miss Hill. She looked at me closely. "You look so worried. What is it?"

"I'm worried about being late home, Miss Hill."

She paused, her tongue feeling round her mouth like a goldfish swimming in a bowl.

"Is everything all right at home?" she asked.

"Oh yes. Fine."

"Your mother . . . ?"

"She's *fine*," I said, my voice loud and cheery, practically bursting into song.

Miss Hill didn't seem convinced. But she made a little shooing gesture of her hand to show I was dismissed. I made a run for it before she could change her mind.

I heard the high school bell go just as I got there. Star was one of the first, without all her friends. She looked at me.

"You've told someone."

"No, I haven't, I swear."

Star nodded. "OK. Sorry. I knew you wouldn't really tell."

We walked home barely talking. When we turned into our road I grabbed Star's hand. She didn't pull away. Her own palm was as sweaty as mine.

DOLPHIN

She was back. I smelt her as soon as we opened the front door. Marigold's sweet strong musky scent. Even if she were wandering round the flat stark naked she'd still spray herself from head to toe with perfume. There was another smell too. The strangest homely mouth-watering smell was coming from the kitchen.

I ran. Marigold was standing at the table, smiling all over her face, kneading dough. I was so happy to see her it didn't even strike me as weird.

"Oh, Marigold," I said, and I flew at her.

"Darling," she said, and she hugged me back, her thin arms strong, though she kept her hands stuck out away from me. They were wearing half the dough like gloves.

"Oh, Marigold," I said again, and I laid my head on her bare shoulder.

The delicate marigold tattoo peeped out from the strap of her vest top, elegantly outlined in black.

"Hey, you're watering my flower!" said Marigold. "Come here, baby."

She took the tea towel between two doughy fingers and dabbed at my face.

"Don't cry, little Dol. What's the matter, eh?"

"What do you think is the matter with her?" said Star, standing in the kitchen door. "She was scared silly because you stayed out all night."

"Still, Marigold's back now," I said quickly, silently begging Star not to spoil it.

Star was staring at Marigold, eyes narrowed.

"Where did all that cooking stuff come from?" she said, pointing at the baking trays and mixing bowls and rolling pins. The whole kitchen was covered with bags of flour and icing sugar and lots of little glinting bottles, ruby red coloring, silver balls, rainbow sprinkles, chocolate dots, like some magical cake factory.

"I just wanted to make you girls cookies," said Marigold, kneading again. "There, I think that's absolutely right now. The first lot went lumpy so I chucked them out. And the second batch were a teeny bit burnt. They've got to be perfect. N-o-w, here comes the best bit."

"Are you making chocolate chip cookies, Marigold?" I asked hopefully.

"Better better better. I'm making you both angel cookies," said Marigold, rolling out the dough and sculpting it into shape. Her fingers were long and deft, working so quickly it was as if she were conjuring the angel out of thin air.

"Angel cookies," I said happily. "Two. Is that their wings? Can mine have long hair?"

"Sure she can," said Marigold. "And if chocolate chip's your favorite your angel can have little chocolate moles all over her!"

We both giggled. Marigold looked up at Star, still hovering in the doorway.

"How would you like your angel to look, Star?"

"I'm not a little kid. How can you *do* this? You go off, you stay out all night, you don't even make it home for breakfast, you crucify Dol all day long at school, and then you bob up again without even an apology, let alone a word of explanation. And you act like you're Mega-Mother of the Year making lousy cookies. Well, count me out. You can have my cookie. And I hope it chokes you."

Star stomped off to our bedroom and slammed the door. The kitchen was suddenly silent. I knew Star was right. I knew I should go after her. I knew by the gleam in Marigold's eye and the frenzy of her fingers and the kitchen clutter that Marigold wasn't really all right at all. This was the start of one of her phases—but I couldn't spoil it.

"Star wants a cookie really," I said.

"Of course she does," said Marigold. "We'll make her a lovely angel, just like yours. And seeing as she's so mad at me we'll make *my* cookie a *fallen* angel. A little devil. With horns and a tail. Do you think that'll make her laugh?"

"You bet."

"You weren't really worried, were you, Dol? Maybe I should have phoned. Why didn't I phone?"

"You couldn't phone. It's been cut off because we didn't pay the bill, remember?" I said, nibbling raw cookie dough.

"Right! So I *couldn't* have phoned, could I?" said Marigold.

"Where were you?" I whispered, so softly that she could pretend she hadn't heard if she wanted.

"Well, I popped out—and then I thought I'd meet up with some of the gang—and then there was a party." Marigold giggled. "You know how I like a party." She was doing the fallen angel now, her fingers skilled even though they were shaking. "And then it got so late and I didn't come back to my girls and I was very bad," said Marigold, and she pointed one finger and smacked the dough devil hard. "Very very bad."

I giggled too but Marigold picked up on my uncertainty.

"Do you think I'm bad, Dol?" she asked, staring at me with her big emerald eyes.

"I think you're the most magic mother in the whole world," I said, dodging the question.

The cookies went into the oven as real works of art—but when we took them out they had sprawled all over the baking tray, their elaborate hairstyles matting, their long-limbed bodies coarsening, their feathery wings fat fans of dough.

"*Oh!*" said Marigold, outraged. "Look what that stupid oven's done to my angels!"

"But they still taste delicious," I said, biting mine quickly and burning my tongue.

"We'll try another batch," said Marigold.

"No, don't. These are fine, really."

"OK, we'll start the cakes now."

"Cakes?"

"Yes, I want to make all sort of cakes. Angel cake and devil cake. And cheesecake and éclairs and carrot cake and doughnuts and every other cake you can think of."

"But—"

"You like cakes, don't you?"

"Yes, I *love* cakes, it's just—"

"We'll make cakes," said Marigold, and she got a new mixing bowl and started.

I helped her for a while and then took the bowl into the bedroom. Star was sitting on the end of her bed doing homework.

"Do you want to lick out the bowl? I've had heaps already," I said, offering it.

"I thought she'd baked cookies."

"This is cake. The cookies went a bit funny."

"Surprise surprise. She's spent a fortune on that kitchen stuff."

"Yes, I know. She shouldn't have. But it was for us."

"You're really a fully paid-up member of the Marigold Fan Club, aren't you?" Star said spitefully.

I blinked at her in surprise. Until recently it had always been Marigold and Star—and then me, trotting along behind, trying to keep up. They were like two lovebirds, bright and beautiful, billing and cooing, while I was a boring old budgie on a perch by myself.

"I don't suppose she's thought to buy any normal food?" said Star, running her finger round and round the bowl.

She'd been biting her nails so badly they were just little slivers surrounded by raw pink flesh.

"Who wants normal food? This is much more fun. Hey, remember that time last summer when it was so hot and Marigold told us to open the fridge and there it was simply *stuffed* with ice cream. Wasn't it wonderful?"

We ate Cornettos and Mars and Soleros and Magnums, one after another after another, and then when they all started to melt Star mixed them all up in the washing-up bowl and said it was ice cream soup.

"We lived on stale bread and carrots all the rest of that week because she'd spent all the welfare check," said Star.

"Yes, but it didn't matter because we'd had the ice cream and that was so lovely. And anyway, you made it a joke with the bread, remember? We broke each slice into little bits and played the duck game? And Marigold carved the carrots too. Remember the totem pole, that was brilliant. And the *rude* one!"

"And she was so hyped up and crazy she carved her thumb too and wouldn't go to Casualty like any normal person, though I suppose they could easily have committed her. And it got all infected and she got really ill, remember, *remember?*" Star said through gritted teeth.

I put my hands over my ears but her voice wriggled through my fingers into my head.

"Shut *up*, Star!"

We never ever used words like "crazy," even when Marigold was at her worst.

"Maybe we *should* have told at school today," Star said.

"*What?*"

"She's starting to get really manic, you know she is. Totally out of it. I don't know what she's going to do

46

next. Neither does she. She might clear off again tonight and not come back for a fortnight."

"No, she won't. She's OK now, she's being lovely."

"Well, make the most of it. You know what she'll get like later on."

"She can't *help* it, Star."

Star had impressed this upon me over and over again. It was like a holy text. You never questioned it. Marigold was sometimes a little bit mad (only you never ever used such a blunt term) but we must never let anyone else find out and we must always remember that Marigold couldn't help it. Her brain was just wired a different way from other people's.

I imagined the ordinary brain, gray and wiggly and dull. Then I thought of Marigold's brain. I pictured it bright pink and purple, glowing inside her head. I could almost see the wires sparking so that silver stars exploded behind her eyes.

"Of course she can help it," Star said. "She could go into hospital and get treatment."

"You're the one that's mad," I said furiously. "You know what it's like in there. It's a torture chamber! You know they put live electric currents through your head and poison you with chemicals so that you're sick and you shake and you can't even remember your own name."

Marigold had told us all about it. She still shook at the memory.

"She was just exaggerating all that stuff."

"No she wasn't! Look, I can remember what she was like then. And you can remember it even better than me because you were older. She *was* sick. She *did* shake. She didn't play any games with us or make up stuff or invent things. She didn't even *look* right, she just wore old jeans and a T-shirt all the time like any old mother."

"That's what I want her to act like. Any old mother," said Star. She pushed the cake bowl away. "I'm fed up eating this muck. I'm going out to McDonald's."

"You haven't got any money."

"Half my school hang out down there. I bet one of the boys will buy me a Coke and some French fries."

It was a pretty safe bet. All the boys thought Star was special. Even though she was only in Year Eight she had a lot of Year Nine and Ten boys keen on her.

I thought about McDonald's and my mouth watered.

"Can I come too?"

At one time Star took me everywhere with her. She didn't question it. I was just part of her routine. But now I had to beg and plead and often she said no. She said no now.

"Why don't you want me anymore?"

"It's not that I don't want you, Dol. I just don't need you to be tagging round after me all the time. No one else has their kid sister hanging around."

"I wouldn't get in the way. I wouldn't even speak to your friends."

"No, Dol," Star said. "You should try to find your own friends."

So Star went out and I stayed in with Marigold and ate raw cake and unrisen cake and burnt cake until I felt sick.

"There! It's been a lovely treat, hasn't it?" Marigold said anxiously.

"Absolutely super-duper," I said.

"I could make some more. There's still heaps of stuff."

"No, I'm really really full. I couldn't eat another thing," I said, wiping crumbs from my greasy lips. My tummy bulged over the top of my tight knickers. I was quite a skinny girl and small for ten but it said 6–8-year-old on the label and the elastic made red ridges on my skin. It looked like I was wearing a transparent pair of pants for ages after I'd taken them off.

"I've saved a slice of each cake for Star, in case she changes her mind," said Marigold. "I thought she'd love a cake treat."

"Don't worry," I said quickly. "She's just being a bit moody."

"She takes after me," said Marigold.

I tried to smile.

"Cheer up, little Dol," said Marigold. "Have some more . . . No. Shut up, Marigold."

She hadn't eaten any cake herself, but she'd drunk several small tumblers of vodka. She poured herself another. She saw my face.

"It's OK, I promise. Just one little weeny drink, that's all. To cheer *me* up. Only maybe we won't tell Star when she comes back," she said, hiding the bottle back in the cupboard under the kitchen sink. The tap was still dripping.

"Stop dripping," said Marigold.

She tried to turn it off more tightly and hurt her hand.

"Ouch!"

"Oh, you poor thing. Don't try anymore. It won't stop. Star says it needs a new washer." I cradled her sore hand in the grubby kitchen towel.

"That's nice, sweetie," Marigold suddenly chuckled. "Look!" She clenched her fist, turning her finger and thumb into a mouth. "It's a little baby. Shhh, little baby." She made the mouth open and wail, and then rocked the towel baby. "It wants something to suck."

I put my finger in the mouth and it smiled convincingly and made little gurgly sounds.

"You're such fun to play with, Marigold."

"Star doesn't play with you much now, does she?"

I sighed. "Not really. She's got her own friends. She says I should get some friends too."

"Maybe she's right," said Marigold. "Would you

like to have some friends round to play, Dol? They could eat up some of the cake."

"No! No, I don't want anyone round."

"Haven't you got a special friend at the moment?"

"Well, I've got lots of friends," I lied. "But no one special."

I'd never been very good at making friends. I had a special friend way back in Year One at Keithstone Primary, a little girl called Diana who had bunches tied with pink bobbles and a Minnie Mouse doll. We sat together and shared wax crayons and plastic scissors and we played skipping in the playground together and we visited the scary smelly toilets together too, waiting outside the door for each other. I get an ache in the chest when I remember Diana and her soft bubble-gum smell and her pink flowery knickers and the way her feet stuck out sideways in her red sandals, just like her own Minnie Mouse. But then we moved, we were always moving in those days, sometimes several times a year, and I never found another Diana. All the children had made their friends when I got to each new school and I was always the odd one out.

Star could arrive in a class and have a whole bunch of kids hanging on her every word by morning break— but she was different. She was born with the knack.

We hadn't moved for ages now, because the Housing Trust found the three of us this flat. We thought at first they were letting us have the whole house because it wasn't really that big, but Mrs. Luft lurked below in the basement flat and Mr. Rowling lived up above us in a studio until he died.

We'd never had such a good home but it meant I was stuck in the worst school I'd ever been at, where they nearly all hated me.

"Who would you *like* to have as your special friend?" Marigold persisted.

I thought it over carefully. I couldn't stand some of the girls, especially Kayleigh and Yvonne. And then there were a lot of girls I didn't even think about much. But I did think about Tasha sometimes. She looked a little like Star, only not quite as pretty of course, but her hair was blond and even longer, way down past her waist. I stared at Tasha's hair when the sun shone through the window and made it gleam like a white waterfall. My hands got sweaty, I wanted to reach out and stroke her hair so much.

"I'd like to be friends with Tasha," I said.

"OK, fine, you can be Tasha's friend," said Marigold, as if it were as simple as that.

"No, I can't. Tasha's got heaps of friends already. And she doesn't even like me," I said, sighing.

"How could anyone not like my little Dol," said Marigold, and she pulled me on her lap and rocked me as if I were a big towel baby. I cuddled up, careful not to lean on the new cross tattoo, which still looked very red and sore. I fingered the blue curve on her bicep. *My* tattoo. It was a beautiful turquoise dolphin arching its back as it skimmed a wave.

"Make her swim," I begged.

Marigold flexed her muscles and the little dolphin swam up and down, up and down.

"I'll make you swim too, *my* little Dolphin," said Marigold, and she rocked me up and down, up and down.

I closed my eyes and imagined cold sea and rainbow spray and dazzling sun as I surfed the waves.

Star came back when we were still cuddled up together. She looked a little wistful.

"Come and join in the cuddle, even though you look too gorgeously grown-up to be true, Star of my heart," said Marigold.

"You've been drinking," Star said coldly, though Marigold's voice wasn't really slurred. "Dol, you should go to bed."

Marigold giggled.

"It's like you're the mummy, Star. Should I go to bed too?"

Star ignored her and sloped off to our bedroom. I followed her. She was sorting through her schoolbooks.

"Are you doing *more* homework? You're already top of your class, aren't you?"

"Yeah, and I'm going to stay top, and pass all my exams and clear off to university as soon as possible. I can't wait to get out of this dump."

"This isn't a dump, it's a *good* flat. It's a posh road. It's the best we've had, you know that."

"It's the best we're ever going to get, with *her*."

"Oh Star, don't. Hey, did you get French fries?"

"Yep. And ice cream."

"Not the sort in the plastic cup, with butterscotch sauce?" I said enviously.

"Yes, it was yummy," said Star. She looked at me. "Look, I'll siphon off some of the money when she gets her next check and I'll take you to McDonald's, OK?"

"Oh, Star, you are kind."

"No, I'm not. Look, it's nothing to get excited about. It's what any other kid takes for granted. You're so weird, Dol. You just accept all this stuff. It's not like you *mind*."

Star never used to mind either. She used to love Marigold, love me, love our life together. She thought everyone else was gray and boring then. We three were the colorful ones, like the glowing pictures inked all over Marigold.

"I wish you were younger again, Star," I said. "You're changing."

"Yes, well, that's what I'm supposed to do. Grow up. You will too. *She's* the only one who won't do anything about growing up."

Star jerked her head in the direction of the kitchen. Marigold was playing an old Emerald City tape too loudly while she clattered kitchen pans, making yet more cakes.

"I hate her," Star whispered.

It was as if she'd spat the words.

"No you don't," I said quickly.

"Yes I do."

"You *love* her."

"She's a lousy useless mother."

"No she's not. She loves us. And she's such fun. She makes up lovely games. And look at her now, she's sorry about last night so she's making us all these cakes."

"Which we don't want. Why can't she make *one* cake, like anyone normal? Why does she go crazy all the time? Ha ha. Easy. Because she *is* crazy."

"Stop it, Star."

"She doesn't love us. If she did, she'd try to get better. She doesn't give a damn about either of us."

Star was wrong.

I came out of school the next day and there was Marigold, waiting for me. She was standing near the other mothers but she stuck right out. Some of the kids in the playground were pointing at her. Even Owly Morris blinked through his bottle-glasses and stood transfixed.

For a moment it was as if I'd borrowed his thick

specs and were seeing Marigold clearly for the first time. I saw a red-haired woman in a halter top and shorts, her white skin vividly tattooed, designs on her arms, her shoulders, her thighs, one ankle, even her foot.

I knew several of the fathers had tattoos. One of the mothers had a tiny butterfly on her shoulder blade. But no one had tattoos like Marigold.

She was beautiful.

She was bizarre.

She didn't seem to notice that none of the mothers were talking to her. She jumped up and down, waving both hands when she saw me.

"Dol! Dolly, hi! Yoo-hoo!"

Now they weren't just staring at Marigold. They were staring at me too.

I felt as if I were on fire. I tried to smile at Marigold as I walked toward her. My lips got stuck on my teeth. I felt as if I were wading through treacle.

"Dol, *quick*!" Marigold shouted.

I got quicker, because she was making such a noise.

"Which one's Tasha?" Marigold asked.

I felt sick. No. Please.

I glanced at Tasha as she crossed the playground, tossing her beautiful hair. I saw her mother, elegant and ordinary in a T-shirt and flowery skirt, her own blond hair tied up in a topknot.

"I can't see her. Maybe she's gone," I gabbled, but Marigold had seen my glance.

"Isn't that her? The one with the hair? Hi, Tasha! Tasha, come over here!"

"Marigold! Shhh! Don't!" I said in agony.

"It's OK, Dol," said Marigold.

It wasn't OK. Tasha stood still, staring. Tasha's mother was frowning. She hurried to Tasha and put her arm round her protectively.

"Hey, wait!" Marigold shouted, rushing over to them. I had to follow her.

"What do you want?" said Tasha's mother.

Her alarm and hostility were so obvious that Marigold couldn't ignore it.

"It's OK, no worries," said Marigold. "I just thought I'd introduce myself. I'm Dolphin's mother. She and Tasha are friends."

"No, we're not," said Tasha.

"We're *not*," I whispered to Marigold.

"Kids!" said Marigold, laughing. "Anyway, we've got a special tea, lots of cakes, all sorts, and we'd like Tasha to come round and play, wouldn't we, Dol?"

"She doesn't want to," I mumbled.

"Of course she does," said Marigold. "What's your favorite cake, Tasha? I'll make you anything you fancy."

"It's very kind of you but I'm afraid Tasha can't possibly come to tea tonight, she has her ballet class," said Tasha's mother. "Come along, Tasha."

"Tomorrow then? How about tomorrow?" said Marigold.

"No, thank you," said Tasha's mother, not even bothering to find another excuse.

She hurried Tasha away as if they'd just witnessed an appalling accident. Marigold stared after them, biting on the back of her hand.

"It's all right," I said quickly. "I don't like her anymore."

"OK, who else shall we ask?" said Marigold.

"No one! Let's go home and eat lots of lovely cake, just us," I said, putting my hand in Marigold's.

We walked away hand in hand, half the school still staring. I blinked my eyes, wishing them greener and greener, real witch's eyes so that I could cast spells with just one flash of my glittering green orbs. Flash. Tasha and her mother lost all their hair and they ran home hiding their pink bald heads. Flash. Kayleigh and Yvonne wet their knickers in front of everyone and waddled away, dripping. Flash. Ronnie Churley tripped over and cried like a baby, boo-hoo, and he had to wear a dinky little baby suit, a pink one with frills. Flash.

But when I looked at Owly Morris his own glasses flashed back at me.

DAISY CHAIN

Marigold wanted us to go to meet Star but I talked her out of it. I knew Star would die if all her new high school friends saw Marigold, especially in her wound-up state.

"No, don't let's hang around Star's school. She's maybe got netball practice today, anyway. Let's just go home."

"I don't want to go home. Boring! Let's have some fun," said Marigold. She put her arm round me, her beautiful bright hair brushing my cheek. "Let's go shopping, eh? Star's been niggle-naggling me about your clothes, telling me you need T-shirts and jeans and sneakers."

"No, I don't. I don't like those sort of clothes, you know I don't," I said, swishing my dusty black velvet skirt and pointing my toes in their 1950s glittery dancing sandals.

"Then let's buy you new clothes you really like. How about your very first pair of high heels?" Marigold suggested.

The idea of owning real high heels dazzled in my head like a firework. But then common sense doused it. I knew I wouldn't be allowed to wear high heels to school. Miss Hill had made enough fuss about my dancing shoes.

"They're not really suitable for school wear. Too . . . flimsy. Can't you wear ordinary sandals?"

I'd looked her straight in the eye.

"I'm afraid we can't afford new shoes for me just at the moment, Miss Hill," I said. "We had to buy these ones secondhand."

I wasn't really lying. The dancing shoes *were* secondhand, but they'd cost a tenner because they were genuine fifties and in beautiful condition.

"Yes, high heels. I'll have some new shoes too. What's Star's size? We'll all have new shoes," Marigold said happily.

"Marigold. We haven't any money. Not till the next check."

"Aha!" said Marigold, and she whipped a shiny plastic card out of the pocket of her shorts.

"But I thought . . . Star said you couldn't use your credit card anymore."

"I got another one, didn't I?" said Marigold, kissing the plastic edge of the card. She tucked it back in her pocket before I could see the name on it. "Let's go shopping, Dolly. Please cheer up. I want to make you *happy.*"

I dithered helplessly. I wanted to go shopping. I knew I only had to mention something casually and Marigold would buy it for me when she was in this mood. It wouldn't just be high heels. It would be strappy shoes too, patent party shoes, ballet shoes, leather boots. Then we'd get onto clothes and I'd end up with a magic wardrobe. Maybe if I wore designer T-shirts and the right jeans then Tasha would suddenly want to be friends after all.

But I knew Marigold had no money in the bank to pay a credit card bill. If it was *her* credit card. She'd sort of borrowed them from people once or twice before. Star said she could end up in prison. Then what would happen to us?

"I don't want to go shopping. Shopping's boring. Let's . . . let's . . ." I tried desperately to think of something we could do that wouldn't cost any money. "Let's go for a walk along Beech Brook."

"The brook?"

"Yes. You used to take us down by the river when we were little."

"Which river?"

"I don't know. I can't remember the place. But

we used to feed the ducks, you and me and Star. Remember?"

Marigold didn't always remember things but now her face lit up.

"Yes! Yes, we did go, didn't we? Before you went to school. Fancy *you* remembering! You were still at the buggy stage. OK, OK, we'll go and feed the ducks. Right. We need bread."

"What about some of the cakes that didn't turn out so good?"

"Brilliant! We'll give the ducks a party they'll remember." Marigold hugged me. "Hey, those little shoulders are still tense. What's up, Dolly?"

"I'm fine."

"And you really want to feed the ducks?"

"Yes!"

"Then that's what we'll do. Dol . . . I know sometimes, well, I act a bit wild and screw up. But would you say I'm a really bad mother?"

"No, of course not. You're a lovely mother."

"Star said—"

"*Forget* Star. Come on. Let's get that cake."

We rushed home, got great carrier bags of cake, and then walked all the way to Beech Brook. Marigold's high heels started killing her, so she kicked them off and stuffed them in one of the bags. She walked barefoot, her long delicate feet padding lightly over the pavement. She had a yellow and white daisy chain tattooed round her left ankle, with trailing fronds winding down her foot and ending with one more perfect pink-tipped daisy on her big toe. Daisies are powerfully symbolic. A chain is meant to protect you from bad luck. Marigold's daisy chain wasn't always effective, but it would have been mean to point this out.

Beech Brook wasn't quite as I'd hoped. I'd heard Kayleigh and Yvonne talking about having a picnic there and they'd made it sound like the most beautiful place in the world. But the brook seemed to have dried to a trickle, and the remaining water was covered with green scum and foamy where it lapped the bank.

"No ducks," I said, sighing.

"We'll find some," said Marigold. Then she swore violently because she'd stepped into a nettle patch.

"I need a dock leaf to take away the sting," she said, but we couldn't find any dock leaves either.

"No ducks, no docks! Dear oh dear," said Marigold, rubbing the sole of her foot. "I'm going to walk up the bank a bit, in the grass."

She held out her hand and I skipped along beside her, the carrier bag of cakes banging against my leg. Marigold nibbled absentmindedly from one of her own carrier bags. Then she started leaving a little trail of crumbs behind her.

"What's that story where the children get lost in a

63

wood and leave a trail of crumbs?" she said. "It was in some fairy-tale book. I had it when I was your age. I didn't really have any books. Maybe I pinched it from school."

"I don't like fairy stories. The good things happen to the beautiful people and the ugly ones are always the baddies," I said.

"So? You should worry. You're beautiful," said Marigold.

"If this was a fairy story your tongue would go black for telling fibs," I said, but I squeezed her hand.

"Handy Pandy? The children had funny names. I didn't like fairy stories either, it was the pictures I liked. Princesses and mermaids and fairies with long curling hair and swirly dresses—hey, what a great idea for a custom tattoo!"

"Did you go and do some flash work for Steve today?"

"No! Boring!"

"But you promised him."

"I'll go tomorrow. And I can work on a fairy-tale design. A whole back! Great on a woman, with flowery swirls and embellishments."

I sighed. We both knew the only people who wanted custom work at the Rainbow Tattoo Studio were big brawny bikers with a hankering for a skeleton death figure on a Harley-Davidson, with strictly no flowery swirls.

"I inked the four Teletubbies on my arm in reading today," I said. "They're easy to do because they're round and blobby. I had red, yellow and green felt-tips but not purple so I asked Owly Morris for a loan of his. He's got this giant set of Caran d'Ache."

"Howly?"

"No. Owly. Because he wears really thick specs. Though he does go howly too sometimes. He gets teased an awful lot."

"Poor little guy. Do you get teased too, Dol?"

"No. I don't wear specs, do I?" I said hurriedly. "I had all four Teletubbies just right but then Miss Hill saw and made me go and wash my arms. I can't *stick* Miss Hill."

I flashed my witch eyes and twitched my black skirt and inflated Miss Hill into a gigantic gray Teletubby with a corkscrew aerial sticking out of her head.

"There was a wicked witch in this story and she captured the children," said Marigold.

"I know. I remember it now. Star read it to me when I was little. It was scary," I said.

"Yeah, that witch was *seriously* scary—but I liked the picture of her, with her big hooky nose and her wild hair and her long gnarled fingers."

"The witch wasn't the really scary bit. It was the mother and father at the beginning. *They* took Hansel and Gretel—*not* Handy and Pandy—they deliberately led them into the wood and got them lost on purpose.

They ran off and left them there. And yet at the end, it was supposed to be a *happy* end, Hansel and Gretel got away from the wicked witch and got all the way back home to their mum and dad and it was like, wow, we're together again, one big happy family."

"I'd never leave you and Star, Dol," said Marigold.

"I know."

"I did stay out—and I have done stuff that's scary—but I wouldn't ever try to lose you."

"I *know*. It's just a stupid fairy story."

"Tell you what. Think what the witch lived in. Wasn't it a little cottage made out of gingerbread?"

"Yes, that was the roof. And there were sugar candy whirly bits."

"And cake. *Cake*, get it? Blow looking for boring old ducks. Let's make our own fairy-tale gingerbread cottage, right?"

"Right right right!"

Marigold tipped all the cake out on the grass and started sorting it into shapes.

"We need a knife," she said. "And something to stick it all together."

"Your wish is my command, O great gingerbread genie," I said, sliding my schoolbag off my shoulder. My ruler made a reasonable knife, even if it was a little blunt, and I had a glue stick to gum everything together.

I sat cross-legged on the grass watching Marigold's long white fingers whisking a cake cottage into shape. I nibbled every now and then.

"Don't eat my roof!" said Marigold, giving me a nudge with her toe. "Look, pick some buttercups and daisies. We could link them together and they'd be great curtains."

I sprang up and searched.

"Come on, Dol. I've built almost an entire house while you've been looking for those curtains," Marigold called.

"I can't find any," I said. "Will these do instead?" I thrust a few bedraggled dandelions at her.

"You're not supposed to pick dandelions. They say you'll wet the bed if you do," said Marigold, laughing. Then she saw my face.

"Oh, Dol. I'm teasing. You haven't wet the bed for *ages*."

"Shhh!" I said, looking round, terrified in case anyone from school might be nearby.

"It's OK." Marigold carefully fashioned a twirly sponge chimney with her sharp fingernails. "I was in one foster home where the mother used to put the sheets over my head if I wet them. These sopping smelly sheets, all in my face, on my hair. And all the other kids laughed."

"That's so *mean*."

"She was a witch," said Marigold, and her finger-nail lost control and sliced the chimney in half. She swore and sighed. "Whoops! And that's the last of the pink sponge. Chimney repair urgently required. Pass us the glue, Dolly."

I kept quiet until the chimney was mended and stuck into place on the sloping yellow roof.

"Were you very unhappy when you were little, Marigold?" I asked.

"Some of the time."

"It must have been horrible not having your mother," I said, snuggling up to her.

"I *had* a mother. She just didn't want me. I didn't care, though. Know what I really did want?" Marigold looked at me, her green eyes very bright. "A sister. I was desperate for a sister. That's why I'm so glad you and Star have each other."

"And we've got you too. You're like our big sister," I said. "Oh, Marigold, you've made such a *lovely* cottage!"

"What about clover leaves for the curtains? They'll look like green velvet, ultrastylish," said Marigold, making arches over the windows with pieces of jam tart. "Stick the little leafy bits at the edge of the white icing."

I managed to find a clover patch and pulled up a whole clump. I squatted down and started gently tearing off each separate leaf.

"I wonder who will live in the cottage. A rabbit?" I said.

"Rabbits would be too big and bumbly. No, two teeny tiny dormice are peeping out at us right this minute, noses twitch twitch twitching, looking at their dream house. If we keep *very* quiet—"

"Hey, look! look!"

"Dol! That's not quiet! You'll scare them all away."

"But *look*!" I held out a clover stalk. "It's a four-leaf clover!"

"Wow!" said Marigold. She looked at it carefully. One of the leaves looked as if it *might* just have torn in two. But Marigold held it up proudly. "A genuine four leaf-clover," she said. "I can feel the luck throbbing through its sap. Lucky lucky lucky Dol." She went to give it back to me.

"No, lucky lucky lucky Marigold," I said, pushing her hand away. "It's yours. And you can't refuse it or it'll muck up the luck."

"Oh well, we can't muck up the luck," said Marigold, and we both giggled. Marigold twiddled the lucky clover in front of her face, and then carefully wrapped it in a tissue and put it in her shorts pocket. "I should be so lucky lucky lucky lucky," she sang.

We stuck the clover curtains into the cottage and then sat in front of it, still and silent, waiting for dormice. We sat there a long time. Several flies and beetles showed an interest, and a butterfly momentarily perched on the twisty chimney.

"I think the dormice are shy," said Marigold.

"They're itching to come and move in, but they can't pluck up the courage to do it while we're watching. So shall we walk on and leave them to it?"

"Right. But what if rabbits come too, or something bigger? A stoat or a fox or something? They'll just knock it flying, won't they?"

"We'll put a hex around it," said Marigold. "Stones!"

We gathered lots of little stones and arranged them in a ring around the cake cottage, leaving just a little mouse-size gap in front of the door.

"Perfect," I said.

"Perfectissimo," said Marigold.

We walked off hand in hand. After ten or twelve paces Marigold looked over her shoulder.

"I saw them! The dormice. They just whisked inside, little paws all scrabbly with excitement," she said, nudging me.

"Really?"

"Really," said Marigold firmly.

We walked on, swinging Marigold's shoes in the empty cake bag. After a while the brook got a bit wider, and when we rounded a bend it got wider still, and the wild vegetation was tamed into parkland.

"Ducks!" said Marigold, nudging me.

"They look very fat overweight ducks, like they need to go on a diet. They don't need cakes," I said.

"And our little dormice needed their home," said Marigold.

"Are they sisters?"

"Sure. Dora and Daphne. Dora's the eldest." Marigold glanced at me. "But Daphne's the prettiest. Her eyes are extra big and beady and her ears are particularly exquisite, very soft and downy on the outside and the most beautiful delicate shell pink inside."

"Daphne sounds lovely. Can she be the cleverest too, even though she's the youngest?"

"You bet. She's the cleverest in the whole class at mouse school. She's very artistic too. She can nibble at a hazelnut, chew chew chew with her sharp teeth and sculpt it into a little statue. She's famous for her wooden cats. She makes them with a roly-poly round base so they tip over with one flick of a paw or tail. All the little mouse babies love to play Tip the Cat."

Marigold went on and on, talking faster and faster, making it all so real I could *see* the mice scampering in front of me. She could be so magic at making things up, much better than Star. Star would rarely play pretend games nowadays. She said she couldn't do it properly anymore. She'd try to pretend but she'd just feel a fool. She couldn't believe it anymore.

I was glad this new mouse game was just for Marigold and me. I realized how rarely we'd been on our own together. It felt wonderful. Marigold wasn't sad or scary at all, she was the best fun ever. Star was so critical nowadays she made Marigold nervous and twitchy. Marigold was just fine with me.

"I love you, Marigold," I said, putting my arm round her slim waist.

"I love you too, Dolly Dolphin," she said, and she hugged me close.

I could feel all the delicate bones of her rib cage through her smooth skin. I carefully patted her long thin arm with the new tattoo etched into her sharply pointed elbow. She seemed too lightly linked together, almost as fragile as the daisy chain round her ankle. Though that wasn't real. It was dyed into her skin forever. I liked the idea of it lasting.

We walked on until the brook became a park stream and we were picking our way through formal gardens. We were miles away from home. Marigold was still engrossed in telling her mouse saga. I didn't want to spoil things by reminding her of the time. Marigold always lived in the moment. She wasn't thinking about Star.

Star would have wondered why I hadn't met her after school. She'd have hung around awhile, then gone home. She'd be there now, wondering what had happened to Marigold and me, waiting and worrying. I knew how awful that was.

I tried hard to think about Dora and Daphne, laughing as Marigold became more outrageous, acting being a mouse herself, her nose twitching, teeth tucked over her lip, her hands curled into mouse paws—but the thought of Star wouldn't go away.

"Star will be wondering where we are," I said at last.

Marigold looked surprised. "I thought she had netball practice."

"Yes, but it's nearly half past five now."

"It's not!"

"And it'll take us hours to walk home."

"We'll get a bus," said Marigold, feeling in her pocket for change. She brought out the tissue containing the four-leaf clover and smiled.

The bus shelter was covered in posters for rock bands. Marigold was in the middle of describing Daphne's summer and winter outfits but she stopped short, distracted.

"What?" I said.

"Emerald City are doing a reunion gig! Oh God. Emerald City! I went to two of their concerts back in the eighties. They were Micky's favorite band."

My tummy tightened. It was usually a danger sign if Marigold started talking about Micky. But she stared at the poster, dazzled. She had the clover in her hand, twirling it round and round in her fingers.

HEART

Star didn't speak to either of us when we got back. I knew she'd been frightened. Her eyes looked pink as if she might have been crying. I felt bad but I'd done my best to keep Marigold away so that Star wouldn't be embarrassed in front of her friends.

I whispered this plaintively in bed at night, but Star simply turned over with a contemptuous sniff. I couldn't stand it when she wouldn't speak to me. It made me feel as if I weren't there. I felt my cold skinny body under the grubby sheet, reassuring myself. I smoothed my silk scarf over my face, snuffling in its soft smell, blowing it gently up and down with each breath. But no matter how I tried to lull myself, I couldn't sleep. I told myself I'd had a lovely time with Marigold and she was fine, but I still felt jangled and tense. I could hear her in the kitchen, wandering restlessly, humming old rock songs, clinking her glass.

I huddled further under the covers and eventually I must have slept because I dreamt I was in the cake cottage with my mouse sister. We sat at our fairy-cake table and nibbled the thick icing with our sharp teeth but it tasted sickly sweet. We washed our paws and whiskers at the cupcake kitchen sink but golden syrup poured out of the taps and we were coated in sweet yellow slime. We crawled stickily up the sponge stairs and curled up in our jam-roll beds but the fruitcake walls all around us started crumbling and the marzipan ceiling suddenly caved in. A huge red vixen was up above us, eyes glinting. She opened her jaws wide and I screamed and screamed.

"Stop it, Dol! You're dreaming," said Star, shaking me.

"Oh, I had such a horrible nightmare! It was so awful." I clutched Star for comfort.

"Don't! You're digging your fingernails right in. They need cutting."

"Can I come into bed with you?"

"No. I'm not talking to you."

"But you are! Oh Star, *please*."

"No! Now shut up and go back to sleep."

"I'm going to Marigold," I said, climbing out of bed. "We had such a great time today. You just wind her up and make her worse. She's fine with me."

Star said nothing. I was forced to pad on out of the bedroom. I went very slowly along the hall, putting the heel of my foot in front of my toes so that I only moved one foot length at a time.

The kitchen light was still on so I went very slowly toward it. Marigold was sitting at the table in her T-shirt and jeans but she was fast asleep, her head slumped, her mouth slightly open. She still had her hand cupped round her glass but it was empty. So was the bottle.

"Marigold?" I whispered. "Marigold, I've had a bad dream."

I took hold of her by the arm. She was very cold.

"Marigold, come to bed. Please."

Marigold groaned but didn't answer. Her eyes were half open and not focusing. I knew there was no point persisting. I went and got her quilt and wrapped it round her. Then I patted her icy hand.

"Night-night, sleep tight, make sure the bugs don't bite," I whispered, and went back to my own bed.

Star still said nothing, but as I felt my way in the dark she reached out and pulled me in with her. She cuddled me close, her lap warm, her arms soft.

She still didn't talk to me the next morning but it didn't matter so much. Marigold was locked in the bathroom being sick so we couldn't have a proper wash and I had to walk to school clenching hard, a pain in my tummy I needed to pee so badly. I was terrified I wouldn't make it, especially the last few seconds as I dashed to the girls' toilets and got the cubicle open and my knickers down—but I was just about OK.

Afterward I had a quick wash in the sink to get the sleep out of my eyes. Kayleigh and Yvonne came in and saw what I was doing.

"Yuck, you're not supposed to wash your face in the school sinks. Here, you haven't been washing your filthy feet in them too, have you, Bottle Nose?" said Kayleigh.

Yvonne giggled at this new nickname for me.

"It's because Bottle Nose lives in a squat. I bet they haven't even *got* a sink at home."

"I do *not* live in a squat, Monkey Bum," I said fiercely, although we'd lived in several squats in the past. One of them didn't have a sink. Someone had smashed it up, and the toilet too, so we had to use a portable potty. That was the squat where Marigold had the worst boyfriend of all . . .

"She's *crying*!" said Kayleigh.

"I am *not* crying, I've got soap in my eyes, so shut up, Camel Breath," I said, wiping my face quick with the back of my hand.

"Bottle Nose lives in a squat!" Yvonne repeated, and another girl came out of a toilet and started joining in, and another silly little kid not even in our year.

"Shut *up*. I do *not*. I live in a dead posh Edwardian house in Beacon Road, so you're totally stupidly moronically mistaken," I said, flicking my limp hair behind my ears and squaring up to them.

"You can't afford to live in a place like Beacon Road," said Kayleigh. "You're a liar, Bottle Nose."

"Well, try following me home and see for yourself," I said.

"*I* don't want to go home with *you*, thanks very much. You're pathetic, asking everyone home with you all the time. I heard your mum ask Tasha to go home with you!" said Kayleigh.

"Her *mum*!" said Yvonne.

They all sniggered. My fists clenched.

"Did you see her tattoos?" said Kayleigh.

"All over her! My mum says tattoos are dead common," said Yvonne.

"Your mum's just jealous of my mum because she's a great fat lump like you," I said, and I shoved her hard in her wobbly stomach.

"Um, you punched her!" said Kayleigh.

"Yeah, and I'll punch you too," I said, and I hit her hard, right on the chin.

Then I marched out of the toilets, the other girls scattering in alarm. Kayleigh and Yvonne told on me. Miss Hill told me off for fighting in front of the whole class.

"It's bad enough when the boys fight but it's appalling when a girl starts using her fists," she said.

"That's sexist," I said, accurately but unwisely.

"Don't be impertinent, Dolphin," she said. She always gave this really hateful sneer when she said my name. Then she went on lecturing me, rolling the words round her mouth as if they were extra-delicious sweets. She loved it when she got an excuse to lay into me. "You must never ever hit anyone, do you understand, Dolphin? It can be very dangerous. You could have done Kayleigh and Yvonne serious harm."

I blinked my witch eyes and inflicted further ultra-serious harm upon them. My fist became iron. It smashed into Yvonne's stomach so hard her intestines spurted out and dangled in the air like a string of sausages. My iron fist punched Kayleigh's jaw so that she swallowed every one of her pearly white teeth and choked. My fist was flexed for serious action now. One blink of my witch eyes and Miss Hill became a giant punch bag. Bam! Pow! Batter! Crunch!

"I hope you're taking this seriously, Dolphin," said Miss Hill.

"Oh yes, I am, Miss Hill," I said.

Zap! Rip! Clunk! Crush!

Kayleigh and Yvonne were onto me at playtime, saying the most awful disgusting stuff, hoping that I'd lose it again and whack them one so I'd get into even more trouble. I knew they'd be even worse at lunchtime, and some of the other kids might join in too. I didn't have to sit with them in the canteen because they nearly all brought packed lunches while I had to eat a yucky school lunch because I got it free. This was an advantage today. I bolted down my sausage and mash and jam tart and custard and rushed outside while they were still chomping their first dinky sandwich. I did a quick survey of the playground and decided there weren't any ultrasafe bolt-holes. I knew one of the teachers would be onto me if I hung about the toilets or the cloakrooms. We weren't allowed inside the classroom.

Then I suddenly had an idea. The library. They'd never think of looking for me there. I wasn't too great at reading.

I hared along the corridor to the library. There was just Mr. Harrison there, sitting at a desk reading his paper, and two little boys mucking around on the computer.

"Hi there. How can I help?" said Mr. Harrison.

I wished I had him as my teacher instead of hateful Miss Hill. Mr. Harrison was youngish and fat and funny. He had very short springy hair like fur and brown beady eyes and he often wore a pullover. He was like a giant teddy bear, but without the growl.

"I think I'd like a book," I said.

"You've come to the right place, Miss . . . ?"

"It's Dolphin. Dolphin Westward."

I waited for the smirk. He certainly smiled.

"Are you gay upon the tropic sea?"

80

I blinked at him. "You what?"

"It's my little weakness, Miss Westward. I spout poetry just as dolphins spout water. I was quoting Wordsworth. You know, the poet who wrote 'Daffodils'?

I didn't know. Mr. Harrison didn't mind. "May I call you Dolphin, Miss Westward?"

I giggled. "You may."

"Would you like me to help you find a particular book? Or do you want to have a good browse and choose for yourself?"

"A good browse, please."

"Certainly. Make yourself at home."

I wandered round the shelves, picking up this book and that book, turning over the pages for the pictures. I *could* read, sort of, but I hated all those thick wodges of print. The words all wiggled on the page and wouldn't make any kind of sense. I looked to see if Mr. Harrison was watching me but he was deep in his paper. I knelt down and poked my way through the picture books for little kids. There was a strange slightly scary one with lots of wild monsters. Marigold would have loved to turn them into a big tattoo. I liked a bright happy book too about a mum and a dad. The colors glowed inside the neat lines of the drawing. I traced round them with my finger. I tried to imagine what it would be like living in a picture-book world where monsters are quelled by a look and you feel safe back in your own bed and you have a polka-dotted mum and a stripy dad with big smiles on their pink faces and they make you laugh.

"What are you reading?"

"Nothing!" I said, shoving both books back on the shelf quickly.

But it was only Owly Morris. *He* wouldn't tease me for looking at picture books.

"Do you have to creep up on me like that?" I said fiercely, just to show him he couldn't mess with me.

"I didn't mean to creep. I have rubber soles on my shoes so they don't make any noise," said Owly. He took a book off the top shelf and opened it up halfway through. There was a bus ticket marking his place.

"Why don't you borrow the book?" I said. "You can take it out the library, can't you?"

"I want to read it *in* the library," said Owly, sitting down at a desk.

"Ah. So you can hide from the others?" I said.

Owly looked at me, his glasses glinting.

"You're hiding too, aren't you?"

"I'm not scared of any of that lot," I said.

"I am," said Owly.

"You ought to learn to stand up to them more. Fight back a bit."

"Look where that got you. In trouble with Miss Hill."

"So?"

"So I don't like getting told off as well as teased."

"Oh yes, well, you're the sickening swotty teacher's pet, aren't you, Howly Owly?"

"Don't call me that. It's not my name."

I thought about it.

"OK. *Oliver*."

"Thank you. Dolphin."

"They're calling me Bottle Nose now. I don't know why. What's wrong with my nose?" I said, rubbing it. "It's not too big and it doesn't have a funny bump."

"Bottlenose dolphin. It's a particular type of dolphin, right? The sort you see performing." Owly made high-pitched dolphin squeaks.

"Right! You'd make a great dolphin, Owly."

"Oliver."

"Sorry, sorry. Do it again."

Oliver whistled and squeaked with gusto, getting so enthusiastic that his glasses steamed up.

"Mr. Morris?" said Mr. Harrison, strolling over. "Are you practicing your one-man-band technique?"

"He's speaking dolphin, Mr. Harrison."

"Oh, I see." Mr. Harrison took a deep breath and then let out an incredible series of squawks that ended with a weird clunk. "That was dolphinese too. Shall I translate? It said, 'Kindly keep quiet in the library or the fat teacher will clump you on the head.'"

Oliver and I giggled.

"No giggling allowed either," said Mr. Harrison,

pretending to be cross. "Here, seeing as you're both interested in dolphins . . . try *reading* about them."

He found us a big book from the nonfiction section and put it in front of us. Big pictures of different dolphins alternated with chunks of text. I looked carefully at the pictures, Oliver read the words. It was quite companionable.

We found the bottlenose dolphin.

"*My* one hasn't got lips like that, though. Mine is much prettier."

"Your one?" said Oliver.

"Oh. Well. There's this picture of one," I said quickly.

"On your mother?"

I hesitated and then nodded.

"I think your mum is *so* beautiful," said Oliver.

I stared at him hard to make sure he wasn't having me on. But Oliver looked totally earnest, blinking rapidly, his long tufty bangs way past the rim of his glasses.

"I think she's beautiful too," I said.

"I especially love her tattoos. They look so special. They're not a bit like the usual ordinary red and blue sort."

"Those are just flash tattoos. You get the designs on the walls of tattoo parlors and they're copied onto your arm. Boring. But my mum has custom tattoos, ones she's designed herself. They're all to commemorate something special in her life."

"And she's got a dolphin to commemorate you?"

"Yep. It's a sort of magic mythical dolphin, not a common old bottlenose."

"Could I . . . could I see it properly?" Oliver asked, breathing hard.

"What? On my mum?" I hesitated. I was used to thinking that Oliver was just awful old Owly. It seemed ultraweird that he was an interesting person inside.

He wasn't a wise choice for a friend. All the other kids teased him, so they'd tease me too. But then they did already.

"Do you want to come round to my house sometime, Oliver?"

"Yes, please!"

"What about your mum? Will she let you?"

"She'll be thrilled that I've got a friend," said Oliver.

"Well . . . not exactly," I said, thinking he was being a bit presumptuous.

"Can I come after school today?" said Oliver.

I thought quickly. I wasn't sure if Marigold would be better yet.

"Maybe not today. My mum gets these moods," I said.

"So does mine," said Oliver. "Headaches and crying and stuff. I have to be extra quiet and make her a cup of tea and give her some aspirin."

"Really?" I said, my heart beating. I hadn't realized other mums could act like that too.

"It's since she and my dad split up. He's got a girl-friend." Oliver whispered the word "girlfriend" as if it were shocking. "I don't like her."

"So? My mum's had lots of boyfriends. Star and me have hated nearly all of them."

"What about your dad? Do you see him on Satur-days?"

"No. I don't ever see him."

"I don't always want to see my dad either," said Oliver. "Dolphin, do you promise I can come to tea at your house?"

"Well. Yes. Sometime. But we don't always have *ordinary* tea. Like it might just be cakes."

"Cool! I love cakes."

"Or fish and chips from the chippy or pizza or something. We don't really have proper cooked teas like other people."

"You are *lucky,*" said Oliver.

He really wasn't taking the mickey.

"Maybe we *are* friends," I said.

I showed off about my new friend Oliver to Star after school. She didn't seem particularly impressed. We were both tense as we opened the front door and went up the stairs. Marigold had spells when she went on drinking every day. But this time she wasn't slumped on the sofa or throwing up in the bathroom. She was singing in the kitchen, her red hair newly washed, her eyes carefully outlined so they looked even bigger, green as green. She was wearing her best black jeans and a tight black top that showed off her figure. Oliver was right. Marigold looked the most beautiful mother in the world.

"Hi, darlings," she said cheerily. "Are you hungry? I've got some juice and chocolate cookies—*shop* ones, Star."

"Great!" I said, starting to gobble straightaway.

Star nibbled her cookie tentatively.

"Good?" said Marigold. "And there's cold chicken and heaps of salad stuff for supper. You'll fix it, won't you, Star?"

Star stopped eating.

"Why? Where are you going?"

"Oh, I thought I'd just have a little evening out, darling. You don't mind, do you?"

"No, of course not," I said quickly.

"Yes. I do mind. *I* was going out," said Star. "I'm meeting some of my friends down at McDonald's."

"Well, how about if you go out tomorrow? It is kind of important that I go tonight," Marigold wheedled.

"It's not fair," said Star, clenching her fists. Her cookie crumbled all over the kitchen floor.

I ate mine up in three bites, even though I was starting to feel sick. I hate rows.

Marigold was doing her best to avoid one.

"I know it's not fair, sweetie," she said, trying to put her arm round Star. Star shrugged her off angrily. "Just this one little night out. Come on. It means so much to me. It *could* even be important to you too, darling."

"How exactly could your going out pubbing and clubbing and getting drunk and making a fool of yourself and picking up strange men be important to me?" said Star.

Her words buzzed round the kitchen like a swarm of angry bees.

"Ouch," said Marigold. She laughed shakily. "Look, Star, this really *is* important. I'm not going to any old pub or club. And I won't get drunk or do anything silly. Look." She took a ticket out of her jeans pocket and waved it. "I'm going to a concert, see?" She'd pulled the lucky four-leaf clover out of her pocket too. It whirled through the air and landed at her feet.

"Don't tread on your clover leaf, Marigold," I said, picking it up for her.

"Thanks, little poppet. I need all the luck I can get," said Marigold, kissing the clover and putting it carefully back.

Star was staring at the ticket.

"You're going to a concert?"

"I wanted to take you two girls too, I know you'd love it, even though you tease me about my musical taste, Star. But they're all sold out. I got this one ticket by a lucky fluke. Well, maybe it was the clover leaf, Dol."

"What concert is it?"

"Emerald City. Remember, we saw the poster?"

"*They're* still playing?" said Star. "They must be positively geriatric by now. Old guys going bald with beer bellies. I'm amazed they're still around."

"This is a reunion concert. They've had separate careers for ages. And you never know—it might be a reunion concert for me too," said Marigold, her eyes glittering.

"What?" said Star.

"Don't you want to meet your father?" said Marigold.

"Oh, please! Do me a favor," said Star.

"Emerald City were his favorite band," said Marigold. "He'll be there. I just know he will. Micky." She always said his name reverently, her eyes shining, as if he were the leader of some strange religious cult and she were his chief worshipper.

She had his name tattooed on her chest, with a swirly Celtic heart beating blackly above her own. Tattooists advise you not to have anyone's name on your body because once it's there you're stuck with it always, unless you laser it away. But Micky's name is engraved forever on Marigold's real heart and no laser in the world could make that ink dissolve.

"Don't you want to meet your dad, Star?" said Marigold.

"You're mad," said Star. She said the forbidden word coldly and deliberately. Marigold flinched. Then she shrugged her shoulders.

"OK. We'll see," she said.

STAR

Star seemed turned into stone. She wouldn't let Marigold kiss her goodbye. I kissed Marigold twice instead.

"You will come back, won't you? You won't stay out all night?" I said, giving her more quick little kisses. Seven for special luck.

"Of course I won't stay out all night, silly Dol," said Marigold. She seemed to have forgotten the other night already. "I'll be back way before twelve, you'll see." She glanced at Star. "With Micky."

She tapped out of the flat in her high heels. She left such a deep silence behind her that we could hear Mrs. Luft moaning from her doorway about stiletto heels marking the stair covering.

Star stood staring into space, gnawing at a hangnail on her thumb. I fidgeted about the room, wondering

90

whether to get started on the chicken and salad. I wasn't hungry but it would be something to do.

"Back before twelve," Star muttered. "Like she's stupid Cinderella. In search of putrid Prince Charming."

"What if she *does* meet Micky, Star?"

"Oh right," said Star, heavily sarcastic. "Whoops. Watch out for that flying pig."

"Wouldn't you like to meet him, though? What would you say?"

"I'd say 'What sort of a father are you, walking out on Marigold and driving her crazy?'" Star paused. "She *is* mad."

"She's not *mad* mad. I mean, she doesn't look loopy and she doesn't hear voices or think she's Pocahontas or Princess Diana. She's just good at making things up."

"She's good at spending heaps of money that we haven't got. She's good at getting drunk. She's good at getting completely nutty ideas into her head. She's good at getting you to think she's Ms. Perfect Mumsie-Wumsie."

"Yes, but she still likes you best. Even now, when you're mean to her. She loves us both equally but you're the special one because you're Micky's child. I wish he was my dad too. She won't ever talk about mine. It's like she can't even be bothered to remember him. She hasn't even commemorated him with a tattoo."

"Well, you can make up for it. Here." Star picked up a pink felt-tip and wrote quickly on my forehead.

"Get off!" I looked in the mirror. I had a "D" and most of an "A" glowing on my skin. "Oh, you pig, Star! What if it doesn't wash off? Miss Hill will go bananas tomorrow."

"Come here. All you need is a bit of spit." Star sucked her finger and then rubbed hard at my forehead. "Is Miss Hill still picking on you?"

"I hate her. And I hate Yvonne and Kayleigh. I hate the whole class. Except for Owly . . . Oliver. He's OK."

"So this Oliver's your boyfriend, right?"

"No!"

"I've got a boyfriend."

"What?"

"It's this boy I met when we were all hanging out at McDonald's. Mark. He's sixteen."

"Sixteen! But that's way too old for you."

"Rubbish. He's great, Dol. Ever so good-looking, with dark hair and amazing eyes, and he's got all these great designer sports clothes. All the other girls are crazy about him but I'm the one he said hi to."

"So you haven't actually been *out* with him?"

"Well, we've met up at McDonald's and we've been down to the recreation center."

"But with all the others."

"He's kissed me."

"Really? You're kidding me, aren't you?"

"No, really. He did it when we were messing

around by the swings and most of his mates were over on the grass kicking a ball about."

"So what was it like?"

Star paused. "I don't know. It was like a kiss."

"Yes, but what did it *feel* like?"

"Slobbery!" said Star, and we both laughed.

"So was it him you were supposed to be meeting tonight?"

"Yep. And some of the others. Janice Taylor will be there too. She's in the year above me at school and she's ever so pretty. She's mad about Mark too. I'm scared she'll get all matey with him if I'm not around."

Star nibbled harder at her thumb, tearing the hangnail until it bled.

"Stop *eating* yourself. OK. You go and see Mark tonight."

"But you're scared on your own."

"I'll be all right."

"*Oh, great!*" Star gave me a big grin and then ran to our room to get ready. "You're sure, Dol?" she called as she changed out of her school uniform.

"Sure I'm sure," I said. "So long as you're not gone for ages."

"I'll be back by ten. Promise. And you can eat all my chicken salad if you want."

I was already wishing I hadn't suggested it. I sat very still, twining my fingers together, wondering what I was going to do. No one to talk to. No television. I could draw, I could look at pictures, I could dress up, I could play hairdresser. I didn't fancy any of these ideas.

"Dol? Don't look like that," said Star, coming back into the living room. She was wearing one of Marigold's tops and she'd outlined her eyes with black stuff. She looked incredibly grown up, a stranger instead of my sister.

"I'm not looking like anything," I said, and I started doodling on the back of my school sketchbook.

I drew a girl with long hair and a tight top. I outlined her eyes and circled her with stars.

"I'm off then," said Star. She peered over my shoulder. "Is that me?"

I grunted.

"I look like I've got two black eyes," she said. "Well. See you when I get back. *Before* ten. You'll be all right, won't you?"

I nodded, not trusting myself to speak.

Star ruffled my hair and then went. I heard the door slam and then the soft pad of her sneakers.

The flat seemed so quiet without her. I wondered about playing some of Marigold's old tapes. But I didn't really want to think about Marigold or I'd start worrying.

I was worrying anyway. I kept looking all round the room, especially behind me. I kept feeling some crazy man was creeping up on me. Or some huge hairy spider was about to crawl over my foot. I pushed my chair right against the wall and tucked my legs up but it didn't make me feel any better.

I drew someone else beside Star. Small ugly fish face with a bottle nose. I drew droplets of water rolling off this little wet drip.

Then I heard footsteps coming up the stairs. My heart started thudding. I gripped the pencil so tightly it made a groove in my hand. I waited for the knock at the door. I decided I wouldn't answer. Marigold owed lots of money to people. Some of the collectors were frightening. Or there were old boyfriends. Especially the scary one.

I was shivering now. I tried to tell myself it was all right. They could bang at the door all night but all I had to do was sit tight. They'd give up and go away eventually.

But there was no knock. I listened hard. Had I imagined footsteps? Then I heard a scuffle and a key in the lock. They had a key! Some of the boyfriends had keys! And now he was letting himself in and I was here all alone. . . .

The front door banged and the footsteps came down the hall. I bit hard on my fist, too scared to try to hide or run.

"Dol?" Star walked into the room and stared at me. "Dol, what's happened?"

"Oh, Star! You scared me so," I said, leaping up and

giving her a punch—and then a hug. "What are you doing back?"

"I got to the end of the road and then I felt a bit mean about leaving you."

"I'm all right."

"Oh yes, sure! You're practically wetting yourself. Come on."

"What?"

"You come with me."

"To meet up with your friends?"

"Yep."

"But you said—"

"And *now* I'm saying you can come. Only not in that awful old dress. Put your jeans on."

"OK," I said happily.

Star leant me one of her T-shirts and I tied my hair up on top of my head to try to make me look a bit older. It stuck straight up like Dipsy's aerial.

"Maybe I look better with it down," I said. "What do you think, Star?"

"It looks fine," she said. "Come *on* or it won't be worth going. Now don't mess about or say anything stupid, will you? Don't act weird. Just try to be normal."

I didn't really know *how* to be normal but it didn't matter. When we got down to the town and joined up with all the crowd outside McDonald's no one was remotely interested in me. They didn't seem particularly interested in Star either. Janice Taylor and the other girls didn't even bother to say hello. The younger boys grinned at Star and jostled around in front of each other but the older cooler guys didn't give her a glance. I sussed out which one was Mark right away but he seemed caught up in some long discussion with his mates.

Star went and stood as near him as she could. I lurked behind her. My tummy was rumbling. I wondered why nobody wanted to go inside McDonald's and start eating. I thought about the chicken salad at home.

"I'm hungry now," I said hopefully to Star.

She was concentrating so hard on Mark I don't even think she heard me. Every time he burst out laughing she bared her teeth and gave a little copycat snort. When he flicked his long hair back Star's own head twitched. When he stuck one hand on his hip Star's skinny arm could have been his shadow.

Two of the younger boys had a silly fight. One of them barged into her. She dug him hard with her elbow and muttered something sharp.

Mark looked up. "Hey, watch out for Twinkle!"

Twinkle! I waited for Star to knock his teeth down his throat. But she softened into syrup.

"Hi, Mark," she said, in this silly little voice.

He fluttered his fingers at her and then muttered something to his mates. They all burst out laughing.

I don't know if Star heard what he said but she

blushed. She bent her head, hiding in her hair, but she still stood there. Waiting. Eventually, when most of the mates had wandered off inside, Mark put his arm round her.

"Coming in for a bite, Twinkle?"

"Can I just have a few of your chips?"

"Don't you want your own? I'll pay."

"It's ever so sweet of you, Mark," she said, golden syrup practically dribbling down her chin. "Hey, tell you what. Can I have an ice cream sundae?"

"Sure."

She went into McDonald's, her shoulder still wedged under his armpit. She didn't even give me a glance.

I kicked the skirting board of the door. What about *me*? It wasn't fair. Ice cream sundaes were *my* favorite too. Star liked chocolate but I liked butterscotch. My tongue came out of my mouth by itself, it wanted to lick an ice cream so badly.

"Who are you sticking your tongue out at, kid?" said Janice Taylor nastily.

I wagged my tongue as rudely as I could.

"Cheeky little whatsit! Who is she?" said Janice's friend.

"She's that Star's little sister. She hangs around outside our school half the time."

"Right! And Star's the one with all the hair?" She nodded toward Star and Mark, who were up at the counter.

"I don't know what Mark sees in her," said Janice. "She makes me sick the way she simpers at him all the time. Why does he want to hang out with a kid like that?"

The friend whispered in her ear and they both giggled.

I stuck my tongue out at them again, wagged it madly.

"They'll cart you off to a loony bin if you don't watch out," said Janice.

She put her arm round her friend and they walked off together. I shut my tongue away. The words "loony bin" banged in my brain. I bit my tongue hard to distract myself.

"What are you doing?" Star whispered. She hooked me into McDonald's and sat me down at a table in the corner. She put her ice cream sundae in front of me.

"It's yours," she said. "I'm over there with Mark, right?"

She ran back and snuggled up close to him. She didn't have anything to eat for herself. I stared down at the sundae. She'd ordered a butterscotch one too.

I licked it with my sore tongue, savoring every spoonful. I knew Star must be as hungry as me. Every now and then Mark offered her a chip, but he made her beg for them like a little dog. She did it very cutely, head on one side, little pants, hands curled in the air like paws, but it still made my skin crawl.

It was worse afterward. Mark and Star went off down the alleyway at the back of the drugstore. I had to hang around staring at shampoos and specs for ages. I was still hungry and my tongue was throbbing. It was so tiring standing still I eventually slid down the glass and sat on the stone pavement, though the cold came straight through my jeans. It was like sitting on a vast tub of ice cream.

I was shivering when Star came back at last.

"Get up, Dol. You'll get a chill sitting on the pavement."

"Where's Mark?"

"He's gone off to meet up with some more of his mates. What do you think of him, eh? Isn't he fantastic?"

"No."

"Yes he is! He's the most gorgeous-looking boy in the whole town. Everyone wants to go out with him. Janice Taylor is hopping mad."

"What did you do with him?"

"What do you think?" said Star. She saw my face. "It's OK, Dol. Honest. We just snog."

I hated that word. It sounded slimey and piglike. Mark and Star grew snouts and pink piggy flesh and horrible curly tails. I pictured them rootling around each other and felt sick.

"Dol?" Star put her arm round me.

"Get off."

"What's up with you?"

"I don't like the way you are with that Mark."

"You're just jealous."

"I am not! And it's not just with Mark, it's all of that lot. You seem so different."

"It just because I'm older now."

"You're still not old enough to have that Mark slobbering all over you. I'll tell Marigold."

Star laughed. "So what's *she* going to do about it? I'm sure she got up to much more when she was my age."

"Do you think she'll come back tonight? She did promise."

"She promises all the time."

It looked like that night was another broken promise. We got home before ten. We ate our chicken salads. Then we got ready for bed. I liked Star much more when she'd scrubbed all her makeup off and was wearing her old teddy bear nightie. She was in such a good mood she made all the teddies talk to me in different growly voices.

"Remember I had a teddy once? A big yellow one with a tartan jacket," I said, rubbing my silk scarf over my nose. "I wish I still had him."

"I'll get you another one for Christmas."

"No, I don't really want another one. I wish I still had Teddy Jock. And all the other stuff. The old picture books and my Barbie doll with all the special outfits."

"Oh, I loved *my* Barbie. But you cut all their hair. I was ultra-annoyed but then I kind of liked it and I made her little black biker boots out of modeling clay, remember?"

"Yes, but we haven't *got* them. I want them all now. I want . . ." I gestured round our room helplessly.

It was the best room we'd ever had and I loved it. We didn't have any proper curtains or a carpet but Marigold had bought a giant pot of deep blue emulsion and we'd painted the walls and the ceiling and then Marigold had turned the walls into an ocean and painted whales and sharks and a coral reef with mermaids and a whole school of dolphins diving up and down. The ceiling was the sky and Marigold had clung to a stepladder all one day and half the night painting the stars of the Milky Way, Sirius and the Pleiades and the Great Bear and the Little Bear and the big bright North Star but biggest and brightest of all she'd painted the five points of the star symbol on her chest above her heart.

It was the most beautiful room any two girls could have. I didn't really want it cluttered up with moth-eaten old toys. I just wished we'd been able to keep more of our stuff. Sometimes the new expensive things were reclaimed. Sometimes they got stolen. Sometimes we had to do a moonlight flit and travel light.

I thought of all the old toys scattered over half of London and beyond and felt sad.

"I wonder what's happened to them all?" I said.

I imagined them scooped up in a rubbish cart and

spewed out on some awful rubbish dump with smelly takeaway cartons leaking all over them and seagulls pecking at Jock's glass eyes and rats chewing the last of Barbie's hair.

Star let me come into her bed when we heard midnight strike and Marigold still wasn't home. I fell asleep nuzzling into the bears on her back and dreamt we were on a rubbish cart, Star and me, and the dustmen combed Star's hair with their dirty fingers and licked her face clean and stuck her up on the front of the cart as their lucky mascot. But they chucked me out on the rubbish heap and I was stuck in the muck screaming for Marigold but she wouldn't come. She wouldn't come for me no matter how many times I cried her name—

"Marigold!"

"Here I am, Dol. It's OK, I'm here. It's all right, darling. Oh God, it's righter than right! Wake up properly. Star, sweetheart, wake *up!*"

Marigold had put the light on. It was so bright I could see nothing at first. I clung to her, my eyes little cracks in my face. I could smell the drink on her breath but she still seemed fine, though she was trembling. I held her tight but she wasn't concentrating on me.

"Star! Star, sit up, my sweet. There!" Marigold leant across me and brushed Star's hair out of her eyes. "Star, I'd like you to meet someone." Marigold's voice was so shaky with excitement she could hardly get the words out. "It's Micky, Star, your father!"

SORCERESS

We sat bolt upright, blinking. We stared at him. It was as if Princess Diana herself had whizzed down from heaven to see us. Marigold had been telling us about Micky all our lives but we'd never quite believed in him.

"You're really Micky?" Star said, staring at this stranger.

Though he didn't really seem strange. He was tall and thin like Star, with long fair hair that tangled around his shoulders. He had cornflower-blue eyes and a straight nose and a crinkly smile and a dimple in just one of his cheeks. He was wearing a black T-shirt and a black leather jacket and black jeans and black boots. He wore a thin silver cuff on one wrist and an ornate silver ring on either hand.

"Like . . . my dad?" Star whispered.

He didn't look like anyone's dad. He looked like a rock star.

Micky glanced at Marigold. She nodded.

"Like . . . your dad, Star," he said.

"Wow," said Star. "I can't believe it."

"I can't either," said Micky. "I didn't even realize I *was* a dad. This is so amazing. First I meet up with you, Marigold. And now I've got a daughter!" He looked at me for a moment. "Hey, you're not my daughter too, little girl?"

"No, that's Dolphin," said Marigold.

"Hi, Dolphin. Cool name," said Micky. His eyes had already swiveled back to Star. He seemed dazzled by her.

"I told you," Marigold said to Micky. "I told you," Marigold said to Star. She was so excited she was practically jumping up and down in her strappy sandals.

Star and Micky just stared at each other, as if they were learning their looks off by heart. Star and Micky and Marigold seemed caught up in a big rainbow bubble floating right up into the air.

I was outside the bubble. Down on the ground. Not part of the family.

"Do you want to get up, girls?" said Marigold. "I could fix us something to eat. Are you hungry, Micky?"

"We ate the chicken, Dol and me," said Star. "Hey,

how did you meet? I mean, there must have been thousands at the concert."

"Thousands and thousands," said Marigold. "But I found him. I *knew* I would. I even knew where to look for him."

"I know, you looked into your crystal ball," said Micky. Marigold laughed delightedly. "You remembered it!"

She had this beautiful sorceress tattooed right on her stomach, with long swirly hair and flowing robes. She gazed intently into a crystal ball, which was really Marigold's navel, the black outline going neatly all round it to make the crystal globe.

"It was my idea, that sorceress with her crystal ball," said Micky. "Let's see her then."

Marigold pulled up her top, giggling. We got a glimpse too.

"She's great. I do a sorceress too, but she bends the other way and she's more Celtic," said Micky, holding out his ring.

"You made your ring?" said Star.

"Micky has his own jewelry business now," Marigold said proudly. "He does all his own designs."

Micky handed the ring to Star.

"It's beautiful," she said, holding it reverently, examining every detail. I tried to look too, but she nudged me. "You're in my light, Dol." She fingered the intricate design, tracing it delicately. She even felt inside, touching the whorled band still warm from his finger.

"Can I try it on?"

"Sure."

"It's way too big," Star said, as the ring swiveled round and round.

"That's because you're so ultrasmall," said Micky. "Exactly how old are you, Star? Are you really thirteen? You look kind of little."

"Your little girl," Marigold breathed, as if she were saying a prayer.

Star tried so hard to look old for her age that I thought she'd get angry but she didn't seem to mind at all. She looked up at Micky through her blond hair. My chest was so tight I could hardly breathe. I knew I should be happy Star had found her father but I couldn't bear the way he was looking at her.

"I can't believe how lucky I am," said Micky.

Maybe he didn't just mean he was lucky to have discovered a daughter. Maybe he meant he was so glad he had the pretty blond fairy sister for his daughter, not the plain stupid goblin.

"We're all lucky lucky lucky," Marigold chanted, dancing round the room.

She looked so beautiful, her red hair flying, arms up, her body snaking this way and that like the sorceress on her stomach, but Micky gave her an odd little glance.

"Lucky lucky lucky lucky lucky!" Marigold sang.

She saw my face and pulled me out of bed, trying to get me to dance with her. I stumbled and lurched, feeling a fool and worrying about my nightie, which was much too short for serious dancing, and very grubby too.

"Come on, Dol, dance! It's your luck too," said Marigold. "Your special four-leaved clover. Hey, maybe I'll design a new clover tattoo, with four leaves, my new lucky number, four, the perfect balanced number, and we have perfect balance, don't we, darling?" she said, whirling me round faster and faster.

"I think we need to eat, Marigold. You seem ever so slightly and ultradelightfully smashed," said Micky.

"I'm not smashed, I'm not shattered, I'm not crushed, I've been broken into shards but now I'm whole again, as good as new, better than new," Marigold burbled.

"I'll see if I can fix us something," Star said quickly, though we both knew there were just a few shreds of lettuce and only enough bread for tomorrow's breakfast toast.

"How about pizza?" Micky said.

It was the middle of the night but he knew the number of a twenty-four-hour takeaway pizza place and phoned it on his mobile.

"What's your favorite pizza topping, sweetheart?" he asked Star.

"Extra cheese and double pineapple."

He rocked back, miming astonishment.

"Mine too! I just don't *believe* this!"

"It's mine as well," said Marigold, though she didn't even like pizza.

"What about you, Dolphin?"

I didn't know what to say. I liked cheese and pineapple too, it was what we always had, but it would sound so stupid if I asked for it too, like some sad little parrot.

"I want . . . mushroom. And peppers. Please," I said.

It was a mistake. We had to wait ages for the pizzas to arrive. I had that sick shaky feeling I always have when I get up in the night. The savory smell of the pizzas was almost overwhelming. Star and Micky started devouring theirs eagerly, swapping long lists of food likes and dislikes, laughing at every similarity, even the most obvious. Who *doesn't* like chocolate and hate Brussel sprouts?

I realized too late that I hated mushrooms. The ones in my pizza were slimey and gray and half hidden in the pizza toppings. It was as if a little band of slugs had crawled into the box and nestled into a pizza bed. I tried to nibble my way round each one, my throat tense in case I accidentally swallowed one. The peppers weren't much better. They were bright red and green and looked pretty but they tasted hot and horrible.

"Leave it," Star whispered. She looked apologetically at Micky. "She's sleepy."

Marigold was only picking at hers. She went to the cupboard and bent down. She took a long gulp of vodka, her back to us. Perhaps she thought she was being discreet.

I could hardly bear to watch her.

"I'll have some too then," said Micky, shaking his head at her.

"Just a little nightcap," said Marigold. "It's bedtime. Look at poor little Dol, she can't keep her eyes open."

"Well . . . I suppose . . ." Micky swallowed the last of his pizza and stood up. He reached out and touched Star's long shining hair. "When can I come and see you again?" he asked, as if he were dating her.

"What?" said Marigold, shaking her head. She took another drink openly. "Micky, what are you on about? You're not *going*?"

"Sweetheart, it's two in the morning."

"Stop it! You're going to stay forever," said Marigold. "You're staying here with us."

"I'll come back tomorrow," said Micky.

"No!" Marigold said it too loudly. "No, you can't go now!" She was nearly shouting.

Micky gave her that little look again. He stayed on his feet. But then Star reached out and took hold of his hand.

"Please stay," she whispered.

His face softened.

"OK," he said, and I saw him squeeze her hand tight.

If she'd whispered, "Please fly out the window," he'd have soared straight through the glass.

Marigold took him off with her. Star and I went to bed but neither of us could sleep. I tucked myself up tight, my silk scarf over my face.

"I can't believe it," Star whispered.

"I suppose he's . . . like she always said."

"He's *better.* I never believed her. And yet she was right all along. No wonder she's always gone on about him. And he's my *dad.*"

"Yes, but he hasn't been like a dad, has he?" I said, some of the sour feeling in my stomach tainting my words.

"How do you mean?"

"He hasn't been in touch or taken you out or done any dad things, has he? I mean, I'm not criticizing, *my* dad hasn't either, it's just—"

"It's just rubbish," said Star. "Because he didn't even know I existed. You heard him. He was utterly taken aback. I bet he never even knew Marigold was going to have a baby. They must have split up before she told him."

"He left her," I said. I curled up even smaller, pulling the scarf so taut on my face it flattened my nose.

Star didn't answer at first. I wondered if she'd gone to sleep. But about a minute later she said, "He's not going to leave me."

She did go to sleep soon after. I couldn't sleep at all. I could hear Marigold and Micky. I slid right down under the bedclothes, the scarf a silk mask. It wavered and tickled every time I drew breath. I lay there long into the night, breathing in, breathing out.

Star woke me early in the morning.

"What are you doing right down there, Dol? You're mad, you'll suffocate. Come *out*."

"Sleepy."

"Come on, wake up! Don't you remember? My dad's here."

"He might have gone now."

"No, he wouldn't." But there was sudden fear in her voice. She moved off my bed. I heard the soft rustling sound of her brushing her beautiful hair. Then she pattered across the room.

"You can't go and see," I mumbled. "Not if he's with Marigold. She'll get mad."

"He's my *dad*," Star said through her teeth, and she left the room.

I sat up and listened hard. She'd shut our door so I couldn't hear much. Star's voice, whispering. And then his voice too. I felt a stab in my stomach. I'd wanted him to have sneaked off. I knew that was wicked. I felt a second stab because I was such a horrible sister.

I couldn't hear Marigold. But she generally couldn't get up in the morning. Star and Micky seemed to be in the kitchen now. I heard the whine in the pipe when someone turned on the tap. My mouth was dry with the taste of last night's pizza. I wanted a drink of water.

I thought maybe I shouldn't barge in on them. I knew Star would want to be alone with him in the kitchen. But it was my kitchen too. And I was very very thirsty.

I got up and went into the kitchen, feeling shy and stupid. Micky was making a cup of coffee, wearing his black clothes, looking fresh and washed though his cheeks were shadowy with stubble. Star was sitting on the table sipping a glass of water and swinging her bare legs. They were deep in conversation but they both stopped when I appeared.

"I want a drink of water," I said, like a stupid toddler.

"Sure," said Micky, pouring me one. "Now, Star and I were just discussing breakfast."

"We have cornflakes. But there isn't any milk," I said.

"I can go round to the corner shop," said Star. "I think it opens early on Saturdays."

"You can't go out and do the shopping," said Micky fondly.

He looked as if he thought she was too little to shop. I wanted to tell him that Star had done the shopping ever since I could remember. She was much better at it than Marigold. I opened my mouth but Star glared at me. She obviously liked him thinking she was just a dumb little kid.

"I thought we'd go out for breakfast," said Micky.

We blinked at him. You could go out for lunch, out

113

for dinner. We'd never thought about going out for breakfast before.

"Where?" I said. Then I suddenly got hopeful. "How about McDonald's?"

"We don't want burgers, we want breakfast!" said Micky. "I know exactly where we'll go. You two girls get your dresses on. I'll try and wake your mum. She was out for the count when I last looked."

We got ready in no time. Star didn't bother with makeup. She wore her black jeans—to be like him—and she tied a black velvet ribbon round her neck.

"That looks stupid," I said grumpily. The black on her white skin looked beautiful.

I wore my own black embroidered top and a black and white checked skirt that Marigold made me from a thrift shop remnant. She'd embroidered black and white yin and yang signs in some of the squares but she'd got fed up before she'd sewn it up properly and so I had to safety-pin it together. I wanted a black velvet ribbon necklace to set off my outfit too but I couldn't copy Star.

We'd woken Marigold together. She said, "Micky?" even before her eyes were open.

"He's still here. He wants to take us out for breakfast," Star said proudly.

"Great," said Marigold, swinging her legs out of bed. She staggered as she got up. "Oh God," she said, clutching her head. "I feel like death."

She was a long time showering and dressing and

putting on her makeup. When she came into the kitchen at last her face was sickly white, her eyes were bloodshot and her hair hung limply, straggling about her ears. Her cross tattoo still wasn't healing properly and looked raw and scabby. She wore the skimpy sequin top and short skirt she'd had on yesterday. It didn't look right in the morning light.

I looked at her worriedly. Up until that moment I'd always believed Marigold was beautiful. Now I wasn't so sure.

Micky was looking at her too, a little crease in his forehead.

"OK, sweetheart?"

I tried to feel relieved. Sweetheart. He must really care about her then. Although he said it in a casual offhand way, as if it was what he called all his girls.

"Right, Star," he said, putting his arm lightly round her shoulders.

He said her name specially, as if a real little star sparkled on his lips.

He had his car outside, a red Jaguar XJ6. Star squealed when she saw it.

"Oh wow," she said. "I've never been in a Jaguar before."

"Sit in the front with me," said Micky.

Star glanced at Marigold. She nodded and put on her dark glasses.

"Yes, sit beside your dad," she said.

Micky chuckled.

"I can't hear that enough times. Dad! It's so weird too, because this last year or so I've been very conscious of time passing—"

"Like a crossroads!" Marigold said triumphantly, climbing into the car, showing a great deal of her decorated legs. "Oh, Micky, we're soul mates! That's why I had to get the cross. Hey, maybe I'll get Steve to add your name and mine, at the back of the cross? Or maybe in a swirly pattern, joined at each end?"

"Whatever," said Micky. "No, what I was meaning, I'd got to thinking how much I'd like to have a kid, seriously wondering about it, though the idea of little puking babies kind of put me off. And now I can't believe my luck! A beautiful ready-made daughter, the sweetest surprise of my life."

Star giggled as he helped her fix her seat back. She peered over her shoulder and mouthed, "*See!*"

I saw all sorts of things that day. It stopped me enjoying what should have been the most special day of my life because we had so many treats. Micky drove us right to London and we had breakfast in a posh hotel. We had croissants and coffee and this most amazing fizzy drink that was partly orange juice and partly real champagne. I wondered if I was going to get drunk. Star seemed slightly sloshed before she'd had a single sip. She sat close beside Micky and he kept fussing over her food, opening up her little pot of jam and spreading her butter for her.

I spread my own croissant and ate it awkwardly, smearing greasy crumbs all down my black velvet skirt. The bubbles in the Bucks Fizz took me by surprise and I coughed and spluttered. Marigold reached over to thump me on the back and knocked her own coffee over in the process. Star and Micky looked as if they wished they were on their own.

We went to Hamley's in Oxford Street afterward, a special huge toy shop. Micky took us to look at the dolls though even he could see that Star was past that stage. I knew I should be too old for dolls too but I ached with longing as I looked at all the specially designed dolls locked away in glass cases. They had beautiful gentle faces and long long long hair. My fingers itched to comb it. They had wonderful romantic outfits too, hand-sewn smocked dresses and ruched pinafores and perfect little leather boots.

I leaned my forehead on the cold glass and stared at them all, making up names for each one and inventing their personalities. They all reached out for me with their long white fingers. They looked so real I was sure they couldn't be cold and stiff to touch. I chose the one I liked the very best. She had long blond curls and blue eyes and a dress and pinafore outfit the pink and blue of hyacinths, with pink silky socks and blue shoes fastened

117

with little pearl buttons. I called her Natasha and knew she and I could be best friends forever . . .

"Come *on*, Dol," Star said, tugging at my elbow.

When she finally managed to prize me away I left a little blur on the glass where I'd breathed in and out so longingly. Marigold was rushing round all the Barbies, talking in a high-pitched overexcited way, as if she were a little girl herself. She was worse down in the toy animal department, picking up bears and lions and monkeys and making them growl and roar and gibber. I got scared one of the assistants would come over and tell us off. I knew Star was tense too, forever glancing at Micky. He seemed surprised but was quite cool about it. He even did a spot of animal talking himself, making a big gorilla lunge at Star so that she squealed. I hung back, thinking of Natasha upstairs.

"*Dol!* Say thank you to Micky," Marigold said, nudging me.

I hadn't taken it in properly. Micky wanted to buy all three of us a toy animal. He tried to talk Star into having the huge gorilla but she laughed and said he was too scary. She chose a honey-colored teddy bear with a slightly squashed snout and velvet padded paws. Marigold made a much bigger production over her animal, juggling with hippos and pandas and an enormous plush python, but she eventually chose an orange striped tiger with great green eyes.

"It looks exactly like you, Marigold," said Micky. He turned to me. "You must choose too, Dolphin. How *about* a dolphin?"

There were big fat turquoise dolphins with black faces and white zigzag teeth. I didn't like them at all but I felt it might be rude to say so. I was desperate to get Star on her own to see if I could ask for Natasha instead. I knew she'd cost a lot more than a dolphin but Micky obviously had lots of money, and he'd been prepared to buy Star the gorilla, which was nearly two hundred pounds. But Star was his daughter. And she'd eventually chosen a much cheaper teddy.

I didn't dare ask outright for Natasha.

"It's hard to choose. They're all lovely. And the dolls are lovely too," I added, hinting heavily. But no one was really listening to me.

I ended up with a dolphin. It swam around in its Hamleys plastic bag, bumping into my legs at every step, snapping at me with its sinister teeth. Marigold carried her tiger ostentatiously over her shoulder so that people stared at her more than ever. Star held her teddy lightly in the crook of her arm. She had a long conversation with Micky about teddy bears. He had had one special teddy throughout his childhood.

"I've always wanted a special one too," said Star. "And now I've got him."

I made a vomit noise. Star and Micky ignored me.

Marigold was whiter than white, looking as if she might do some real vomiting. She talked nonstop. Micky would nod or comment every now and then but he barely looked at her.

We had lunch in Planet Hollywood and we got three T-shirts and then we went to the game hall and went all round Sega World. I tried counting up in my head how much all this was costing. Maybe Micky was a millionaire?

We went for a walk round Soho afterward. Then we went to Chinatown and Micky bought us embroidered Chinese slippers, black for me, green for Marigold, and ruby red for Star.

We were still very full with lunch but we stopped for cakes in a French tea shop. Marigold didn't order a cake. She had a lemon tea. She kept sipping and sipping it. Maybe she was thirsty because she'd been doing so much talking. I chose a big creamy cake with pink marzipan icing. It was beautiful but I felt embarrassed in case Micky thought I was greedy. He and Star chose strawberry tarts. Star didn't eat her pastry. She just pecked out the big strawberries and relished them, licking them clean of cream and delicately nibbling the red flesh.

Micky watched her with amusement.

"Don't mess around with your cake like that, Star. Eat it up properly," said Marigold.

"Let her eat it how she wants. She's enjoying herself," said Micky.

"You can say that again," said Star. "This is the best day of my life. I don't want it to ever end."

There was a funfair in Leicester Square with one of those mad machines where they strap you in and whirl you round and round.

"Hey, let's have a go!" Marigold yelled.

Micky looked at Star. She pulled a face.

"Hang on, Marigold. The kids will be sick straight after eating those cakes."

"Oh come on! You come with me, Micky," said Marigold. "Do let's, darling. The girls will wave at us, right? Come *on*, let's have some fun!"

Marigold looked as if she was being whirled round right where she was. Her hair stood out, her eyes glittered, her whole body jumped and twitched. She grabbed Micky's arm, trying to pull him.

"I hate those things, babe," said Micky. "And we can't leave the girls standing by themselves, there are all sorts of crazy characters round here. Hey, why don't we all go on the roundabout?"

"Oh *yes*, I love roundabouts," said Star.

"So do I," I said, though no one was listening to me.

I pretended Natasha had kicked her way out of her glass cage with her little blue boots and had run all the way down Regent Street to find me.

"Yes, we love roundabouts, don't we, Dol?" she said, and she put her little hand in mine and jumped up and down, her silky curls flying out round her face.

Marigold was getting in a state and I didn't want to see so I swept Natasha up into my arms and told her that she could come and live with me. I'd undress her and wrap her in my special silk scarf each night and we'd cuddle up in my bed and tell each other secrets and then we'd go to school together each day and all the other girls would want to be Natasha's friend but she wouldn't talk to anyone but me. Well, she might say hi to Owly but absolutely no one else. We'd be work partners and she'd be brilliant at lessons and do all the writing for me and we'd come top all the time. . . .

"For God's sake, Marigold," said Micky, and he shook himself free from her clutching hand.

She stood for a moment, her hand empty. Then she started laughing.

"Well, *I'm* going to have fun," she said, and she dashed off to the whirly machine herself.

Micky looked at Star.

"Is she often like this?" he said.

Star hesitated. "She's OK," she said eventually. "Can we go on the roundabout?"

I chose a black horse with red nostrils and a purple saddle. I sat behind the twisted gold rail so that Natasha could sit in the front. Star chose a white horse with a scarlet saddle. She sat at the front. Micky got up behind her. I watched them and felt giddy even though the roundabout hadn't started. I looked across the square for Marigold. She was sitting up on the machine, showing a lot of her legs, still clutching her tiger. There were lots of other people strapped in too but the seats either side of her were empty.

The roundabout started. Each time it twirled me past the machine I craned my neck to spot her. It had started hurtling violently backward and forward and round and round. Everyone was screaming. Marigold's mouth was a huge O as she screamed louder than anyone.

I gripped the rail until my hands hurt. The roundabout slowed down but Micky paid for us to have two more turns. He and Star were talking all the time. It was as if their white horse had galloped off the roundabout and carried them far away.

I tried to talk to Natasha but I couldn't make it work anymore. I was on a horse by myself and it was getting dark and the day was about to end and I didn't know what was going to happen and I was scared.

Marigold was much more scared than me. She was shaking all over when she stepped off that stupid machine. Micky had to put his arm round her to support her. She leant back against him, nuzzling into his neck.

"Come on, I think it's time we went home," said Micky.

"Your home?" said Marigold.

"No, not mine," said Micky. "You know I live in Brighton now."

"Our home," said Marigold. "Never mind. Just so long as we're together. Oh, Micky, I can't believe we've found each other again. And we're going to have fun fun fun fun."

I don't know who she was kidding. Maybe not even herself. She chatted and sang and bounced round all the way home, but she sounded desperate. Micky waited to announce the obvious until he'd drawn up outside our house. He made sure we were out of the car.

"I have to go back now. But it's been a truly great day and I'll come again really soon."

He gave me a little squeeze on the shoulder, he gave Star a shy kiss on the cheek and then he paused helplessly in front of Marigold. She'd started to cry.

"No tears, babe. I'll be back soon, I promise," he said, giving her a kiss on her cheek as if she were a child like us.

Then he jumped back into his car and drove off. I looked at Star. She watched the car until it was out of sight. She went on watching, as if she could still see it. She wasn't crying like Marigold. Her face was carefully expressionless but her eyes were shining.

EYE

Micky sent presents every day. Not just for Star. For me too—and Marigold. Some were funny little presents, like a dainty flowery hankie for Star and me and a great big giant red and white spotted hankie for Marigold to mop up all her tears. Some were practical. He sent a mobile phone because he knew our own phone had been cut off. Some were expensive, necklaces in little black velvet drawstring bags. I had a little silver dolphin on a silver chain. I wished I didn't always get stuck with dolphins. Marigold had a big droplet of amber almost the exact orange of her hair. Star had a round black shiny stone that gleamed like a star whenever it caught the light. It hung on a narrow black velvet ribbon.

"Black onyx," said Marigold.

"No. It's a star sapphire," said Star, saying the name as if it were holy.

"It's not. Sapphires are blue, everyone knows that," I said.

"*Star* sapphires are different. They're black and they look like they've got a star trapped inside. Micky told me," said Star.

She seemed to have managed to do a lot of talking with Micky. She sometimes sneaked the mobile phone into her schoolbag before Marigold was up. She certainly didn't seem surprised at the present that arrived early on Saturday morning. It was two children's tickets to Brighton and back, dated that day.

"What are they?" I said stupidly.

"Oh, Dol, wake up. Come on. Let's hurry. Pack your nightie, we're staying overnight. Ugh, on second thought, don't, it's way too gungy. You'd better just sleep in your knickers. Now, toothbrush, hairbrush, clean underwear . . ." Star's things were all to hand, suspiciously spick and span. She'd known about this all right.

"Isn't there another ticket?" I asked, looking in the envelope.

"They're both here, with Micky's note," said Star.

"No, I mean a third ticket. For Marigold."

"For me?" said Marigold, stumbling into our bedroom.

She looked pretty hopeless. She'd been drinking a

lot since last Saturday, and talking nonstop about Micky. Talking nonstop *to* him too, whenever she could grab the phone away from Star.

Star shook her head. Marigold went white and ran to the bathroom. We heard her being sick.

"She's upset," I said.

"She's drunk too much," said Star. "Please hurry up, Dol. It'll be much easier if we go now. We can phone Micky from Victoria to say which train we're getting and he'll meet us."

"We can't just leave her!"

"We can. She leaves us," said Star.

This was true enough. But it still seemed too terrible a thing to do to her.

She looked worse then ever when she came out of the bathroom at last. She was shivering in her petticoat, holding her own arms tight. She looked at the things Star was quickly stuffing in her shoulder bag.

"We're going to Brighton for the weekend," Marigold said. "Micky told me on the phone."

"It's just Dol and me," said Star. Her voice wobbled even though her face was firm.

"And me," said Marigold. "Whew! I don't know what's up with me. Some tummy bug. Hope you girls don't get it. *Right!* I'd better get my act together and get packing."

"There are just two tickets, Marigold. One for Dol and one for me," said Star.

"Oh," said Marigold, taking the envelope and peering inside, then tearing it right open. "Well, it can't be helped. I don't mind forking out for my own ticket."

"Marigold. It's just Dol and me that are invited. I thought Micky explained."

"Explained what?" I said.

"We're staying with him."

"Well, I can stay with him too," said Marigold.

Star sighed. She clenched her fists. She swallowed.

"His girlfriend will be there."

"His girlfriend?" I said, twitching.

"*I'm* his girlfriend," said Marigold, running her fingers through her hair, trying to twist it into place.

"He's got this other girlfriend who lives with him, Marigold. Sîan."

"Sîan?" said Marigold, as if it were some disgusting swear word.

"He said he told you all about her."

"Yes, he did mention some girl. But he's the only guy I've ever truly loved, so I don't care if he's had a few girls since. He wouldn't be human if he hadn't. But I'm the one he went looking for. I'm the mother of his *child*. Of course I've got to come too. I've got to, haven't I, to see you're both all right."

"We'll be fine, Marigold," said Star. "Dol and I had better get going. Micky said we should try and get the ten o'clock train."

"Please. Wait for me. Let me come too," Marigold said, rushing into her bedroom, putting her best beaded cardigan on over her old petticoat but buttoning it up all wrong so that it hung lopsidedly.

"Why can't she come too?" I growled at Star.

"There's nowhere for her to stay. Micky said."

"Micky said, Micky said. I'm getting a bit sick of your Micky," I said. "He doesn't own the railways. He doesn't own the whole of Brighton."

"He does own his own flat. It's very tiny. He's bought these two camp beds for us and we'll be sleeping in his living room and he and Sîan have the bedroom. There isn't room for Marigold."

"I could sleep on his sofa. Or this Sîan could. Look, if I'm going she doesn't *need* to be there, acting like a nanny or whatever."

"She lives there most of the time. She and Micky have been together for more than two years."

"I'm his girlfriend," said Marigold, sticking her bare feet in her high heels and trying to pull her cardigan straight.

"Don't be so stupid, Marigold. You only knew him a few *weeks*. He told me."

"He stayed here last Saturday night!"

"Because he wanted to see *me*!" Star shouted. "And he wants to see me this weekend too and I'm not going to let you muck it all up. You're *not* coming."

"I'm not coming either," I said.

They both blinked.

"I'm not coming," I repeated.

"Don't be daft, Dol. Of course you're coming."

"Micky doesn't want to see me. And I don't want to see him either. I think he's horrible. And I think you're horrible too, Star. Marigold and me will stay home. You go off to Brighton with your precious Micky. See if we care."

"Right," said Star. "*Right.*"

She picked up her bag and walked out of the room. We heard our door slam, footsteps hurrying downstairs, and then the thunk of the front door closing.

It was very quiet in our flat. Marigold stood half dressed, shivering, still tugging at her cardigan.

"Dol?" she said, tears brimming.

"It's OK," I said. "Look, you've buttoned yourself all skew-whiff. Come here."

I did her buttons up properly. She still looked dazed, tears dripping down her face.

"We'll have a lovely time, just you and me," I said. I hugged her tight, so that all the little beads in her cardigan dug in hard against my skin.

I couldn't help hoping that Star would suddenly come rushing back. She'd say Marigold could come too. She'd insist I go with her. She'd stay at home with us.

She didn't do any of these things.

Marigold and I were left on our own. I wanted her

to be pleased with me that I hadn't gone with Star. But she started to get things twisted in her head, acting as if it were *my* fault she wasn't invited to Brighton.

I argued with her and she got really angry and started yelling, screaming as if she'd never stop, her eyes little green slits, her mouth a great red cavern, spittle running down her chin. She kept waving her arms in the air and I was scared she was going to hit me even though she'd never smacked me in my life. I tried talking back to her but she was making so much noise she didn't hear me.

There was a big thumping at our door. Marigold took no notice of that either, so I didn't answer it. I knew who it would be.

Mrs. Luft started hissing through the letterbox.

"If you don't stop that crazy noise I'll call the police and they'll get you carted off to the loony bin where you belong!"

Marigold heard that. She sprang to the door and flung it open. Mrs. Luft staggered backward, almost falling over. Marigold's arms were still flailing.

"Don't, Marigold!" I screamed.

Marigold got stuck in space, arms up, on the tips of her toes, mouth stretched in a shriek.

"Don't!" I said. "Don't!"

Marigold looked at me as if she could see me properly at last. She dropped her arms and slumped against the wall, breathing heavily.

Mrs. Luft backed away, still in a crouched position.

"She's crazy! A real crazy woman, acting totally demented. And her with two dependent kiddies!" she muttered.

"We're fine," I said. "My mum was just mad at me because I did something ever so naughty. She shouted at me. So what? And we're not just dependent on Marigold anyway, we've got a father, haven't we, Marigold? Star's with him now and if he thinks you've been saying wicked things about my mum like she's mad then he'll sue you for slander, just you wait and see, you mean old rat bag."

Mrs. Luft straightened up.

"I'm not indulging in a common brawl. You belong in the gutter, all of you. Now keep your voice *down* or I really will call the police."

I shut the door on her. I felt the blood zipping round my body as if I'd been running a race. I wanted Marigold to clap me on the back and congratulate me but she seemed out of it again. She rolled up her sleeve and started fingering her new cross tattoo, scraping along its lines with her nails.

"Don't! You'll get it infected, picking at it like that."

I got her antiseptic cream and she rubbed it in slowly. It seemed to soothe her. She got washed and properly dressed. I did her hair for her. I combed it up into a chic plait and anchored it with my green clasp.

"Close your eyes," I said, and I sprayed her hair thoroughly to keep every single tendril in place.

Marigold's third eye stared back at me, unblinking. She'd had another big green eye tattooed at the back of her neck. It was usually hidden by her sweep of hair. It was a bit startling seeing it looking at me like that. When I was in Year One at my first primary school—I can't even remember its name, I went to so many different schools—but anyway this teacher used to cluck at us if we were naughty and say she needed eyes in the back of her head to see what we were all up to. I told her my mum *had* an eye at the back of her neck, a big green one, and she said, "Yes, dear," as if she didn't believe a word of it.

I put my finger out and touched the green skin. The eye still didn't blink but I could feel Marigold quivering.

"Don't poke me in the eye," she said.

It was our old old joke. It was great to hear her say it. She seemed to have calmed down. I could still hear all that shouting in my head and it was still scary. Maybe it was good she'd got it all out of her system. Now she wasn't mad at me anymore.

"What shall we do today, Marigold, you and me?"

Big mistake.

"Do?" said Marigold. "We're going to Brighton."

I did my best to talk her out of it. We didn't know where Micky lived for a start.

"We'll find it. I'll know as soon as I'm near it," Marigold said.

"*How* will you know?" I looked at the mobile phone. "I suppose you could always phone and ask?"

But she didn't know the number. Micky had always phoned her.

Star knew the number. She'd kept it to herself.

We both stared at the phone as if it could dial the number by itself. It suddenly started ringing and we jumped as if it were alive. Then we both made a grab for it. I was quicker.

"Is that you, Dol?" It was Star, from a phone booth. I could hear announcements in the background.

"Are you at the station?"

"Yes. Listen. How is she?"

"She's . . . OK," I said. I didn't want to tell Star about Marigold's shouting fit. And it was all over now.

"You're sure? Look, I've got to get the train in a minute, but I just wanted to check."

"Star, wait for us. We're coming to Brighton too."

"No, not with Marigold you can't. Don't let her."

"Star, *please.*"

"O—o—h." Then there was a little sound like a sob. "I wish I knew what to do," she said. "Why couldn't you have come with me in the first place? Oh, Dol, is she really OK? Look, I have to go, I'll miss the train. I have to see Micky. He's my *father.*"

"What's his phone number, Star?"

"What?"

"The number. I need the number."

"No. I can't give it to you. I'm not allowed," said Star. "I'll phone you. I'll phone this evening, right? And I'll be back tomorrow."

Marigold grabbed the phone from me.

"Star, sweetie, I have to talk to Micky. It's a terrible emergency. Please give me the number right this minute."

Star rang off. Marigold screwed up her face in anguish. A strand of hair escaped and dangled down round her ear. I tried to pin it back into place.

"We can ring directory inquiries," I said. "Give them Micky's name."

"Brilliant!" said Marigold.

But Micky was unlisted.

"It doesn't matter," said Marigold. "I don't need it. I know all the *real* things about him, the way his eyes crinkle when he smiles, the freckles on his back, the way he sings in the shower, the music he's crazy about. There, Dol, I knew he'd be at the Emerald City concert. I found him there. I just walked straight up to him. We'll go to Brighton and we'll walk straight there and he'll be so glad to see us. It'll be just like last Saturday. We had such a magic time, didn't we? The four of us. Just like a family."

"But Star says he's got this Sîan."

"She's nothing. We'll get rid of her," said Marigold. "Come on, Dol. We're going to Brighton. What were you playing at, wasting all this time, having that silly tantrum?"

I stared at her. Did she *really* have it so mixed up in her head that she thought *I'd* done the shouting? She didn't quite meet my eyes. She turned her back so that the third eye could gaze at me steadily.

So we went to Brighton. We used my ticket. Marigold used her new credit card for hers. It was another scary thing to worry about.

I couldn't remember if I'd ever been to Brighton before. Marigold stepped out smartly the moment we got off the train but she didn't seem to know her way round either. It wasn't too difficult to walk toward the seafront because you could tell by the glint in the distance. It was further than it looked. Marigold was wearing her high heels.

"We'll get a taxi," she said, spotting one.

The taxi stopped and the driver stared at her.

"Take us to Micky's place," Marigold said, climbing into the back of the cab.

"Where?"

"*Micky's* place."

"Is that a club or a pub or what? What's the address?"

"I'm not too sure. If you could drive us around for a bit I'm sure I'll recognize it."

"Have you got cash, lady?"

"Of course I have. Well, credit card."

"No, thanks. Out you get. And you, little girl. I'm not taking you on a tour round blooming Brighton. You're crazy."

"What did you call me?" said Marigold.

I had to haul her out of the cab quick. We walked after that. Down to the seafront. There was no sand but the sea was a bright turquoise blue and the pier had a huge glitter ball that sparkled in the sunshine. Marigold started to sparkle too. She caught my hand and we went on the pier and she found a booth where they do astrology charts to see if you're compatible with your partner. She knew Micky's birth date even though she didn't know his phone number or address, so she used up the last of our cash seeing if they were soul mates.

The computer printout reckoned they were 75% compatible, much higher than average. Marigold read it three times, a huge smile on her face. Then we went through the amusement arcade to the end of the pier and back. I wished she'd left some cash so we could have a go at grabbing a bright green teddy or a fluffy panda with a spotted bow tie out of the machine. I'd have loved an ice cream too. It was way past lunchtime. Marigold rarely got hungry when she was in one of her states.

There was a fish and chip place in the middle of the pier. The smell made me suck in my cheeks. There were people sitting in a long line of deck chairs nibbling bits of batter and chomping chips. One thin girl barely touched her polystyrene platter, just throwing the odd chip to the seagulls. Then she went off with her boyfriend. I stared after them. I stared at her fish and chips. There were seagulls with beady eyes and sharp orange beaks perching on the pier railings, waiting. I got there first, snatching the platter up and tucking in.

"Dol!" said Marigold, but she didn't stop me.

She stared way into the distance, eyes narrowed. Every time she spotted anyone with fair hair she tensed up, her hand clasping my greasy fingers, but so far we hadn't caught a glimpse of Micky and Star.

"But we *will* find them," said Marigold.

We walked and walked and walked. Marigold had such bad blisters she stuffed old tissues between her straps and her feet. We went all over a big modern shopping center asking in all the jewelry shops, but no one knew Micky or his work.

"They're all too modern, too tacky, too chain store," said Marigold.

We went round and round little winding lanes full of antique jewelry shops.

"Too old," said Marigold, after we'd gone in and out of every one.

We walked further and found small lively streets with people plaiting hair and playing penny whistles and selling amber off stalls.

"This is more like it," said Marigold.

We went into several jewelry shops. We couldn't see any rings like the one he'd been wearing and there were no necklaces like ours. No one knew Micky—or if they did, they weren't letting on to us.

"We're not going to find him, Marigold," I said, undoing my shoes and arching my poor sore feet.

"Of *course* we're going to find him," said Marigold, pulling me after her before I'd even got my shoes back on properly.

We tramped round all over again, until the shops started shutting.

"Can't we go home now?"

"We're not going home until we join up with Micky and Star," said Marigold.

She seemed to think if she said it enough times it would somehow come true. She kept slowing down when we went past pubs. I knew she was longing for a drink. I was terribly thirsty myself. I tried drinking from the cold water tap in a ladies' loo but it was hard gulping it down. Most of the water splashed my front, making my T-shirt uncomfortably sodden. It was starting to get cold, the wind blowing off the sea.

"*Please* let's go home," I begged.

"Just stop it, Dol. You've got to stop being so negative. Maybe it's your fault we've not found them yet."

I was scared she was starting to get angry again. I was tired and hungry and cold and my feet hurt. I just couldn't hold on anymore. I burst into tears, great gulpy sobs like a baby.

"Stop it," said Marigold.

I couldn't.

"*Stop it!*" she said. "Look, it'll be all right when we find them. Micky will take us out for a meal and we'll have such a great time. It will be beautiful, I promise. But you've got to shut up now, Dol. People are staring at us. We'll just walk a little further. I bet we suddenly stumble on them in the next street. I just know we'll find them if we only try hard enough."

"That's crazy," I sobbed.

Marigold slapped me hard across the cheek. I reeled back, catching my breath. Marigold seemed stunned too. She looked at her own hand as if she couldn't believe what she'd done.

Someone said loudly, "Fancy slapping your child like that!"

"She ought to be reported," said another.

Then someone tugged at my arm.

"Are you all right, dear?"

I stared at them. I stared at Marigold.

"Quick, Dol," said Marigold, catching hold of my hand.

She started running, pulling me with her. Someone shouted after us but no one tried to follow. When we were halfway up the street Marigold pulled me into a shop doorway.

"I'm sorry, Dol, I'm so sorry," she said, starting to cry herself. "I didn't mean to hit you. Oh God, I can't

see in this light. Is your cheek all red? You poor poor little thing. I was so mean to you. Here, hit me back.
Really slap my face. Go for it!"

She picked up my hand and tried to make me hit
her. My arm flopped back to its side.

"I don't want to hurt you," I said, sniffing.

"Oh, don't. That makes me feel worse," said
Marigold, crying harder. She cried like a little girl, her
mouth open, snot running down her nose.

I fumbled in her bag and found a tissue.

"Here," I said, wiping her face carefully.

"It's like you're the mum," Marigold wept.

It was a game she sometimes liked to play. I decided it was my best chance of getting us home.

"Yes, I'm the mum and you're my little girl
Marigold. Dear dear, you've got yourself in such a silly
state, darling. Let Mummy wipe your nose again," I
said. "Now, come along with me, there's a good girl.
I'll tell you a story as we go, right, precious?"

"Yes, Mum," said Marigold in a little girl's voice.

"OK then, darling. Well. Once upon a time there
was a little baby girl called Marigold and she had eyes
the color of emeralds and hair the color of the setting
sun, and she got stolen away by evil people . . ."

It was an old old story, one that Marigold had made
up herself, but she listened as if she were hearing it for
the first time. We walked on uphill, and I hoped and

141

hoped we were going in the direction of the station. Marigold stumbled once and twisted her ankle. I put my arm round her. She snuggled in. I felt as if I really were the mother and she were my little girl. I wished I could lift her right up in my arms and carry her. She was crying again, tears dribbling down her cheeks.

"We're giving up, aren't we?" she said.

"No, darling, of course we're not giving up. We'll come back lots and lots and we'll find them and it'll be lovely, like you said. But we're tired now, you're very very tired, so Mummy's going to get you home and put you to bed and cuddle you to sleep."

Marigold stopped. I thought she was going to stop the game, stop me. I waited for her to get angry. She looked at me and it was as if she were looking right through my eyes into my head at all the worries inside.

"Oh, Dol," she said. She sighed as if all the breath had been kicked out of her. "Oh, Dol, why do I do this to you?"

She came to the station and we caught the train. She fell asleep. I put my arm round her and let her rest her head on my still-damp chest. The ticket man came and I had to wake her, but she was OK with him, even chatting him up a little bit. He had tattoos on his arms, simple heart and dagger flash work. He looked at Marigold's skin with awe.

When we got back home at long last the phone was ringing. Ringing and ringing.

Star sounded frantic when I spoke.

"Oh Dol, I've been so scared! Why didn't you *answer?*"

"We've been out."

"Didn't you take the phone with you?"

"We didn't think about it."

"That was the *point*. It's a mobile, right? Oh God, you're so stupid. Are you all right? Is Marigold OK? Where have you *been?*"

Star paused. I paused too. Marigold stood watching, biting her finger.

"Oh no. You haven't been to Brighton looking for us, have you?"

"Of course not," I said quickly.

"Yes, you have! You should have stopped her. Look, Dol, even if she found him it wouldn't be any use. Micky's got Sîan. He doesn't want anything to do with Marigold anymore anyway. Listen, he thinks she needs treatment. He says it isn't all horrible and electric shock stuff like Marigold goes on about. He says she can just take this drug and it'll calm her down. But he says she shouldn't be looking after us when she can't even look after herself."

I was holding the phone so hard against my ear that I was making grooves in my skin. Star's voice still leaked out of a corner. Marigold could hear every word.

"Shut up, Star!"

"Micky's dead worried about you, Dol. You should

have come with me. I'm telling you, he thinks she's really crazy."

I cut off the call. Marigold stared into space. Then she dragged herself into her room and fell on her bed. She wept into the pillow where Micky had lain, her skirt rucked up, her poor sore heels blistered and bleeding. Her hair straggled down from its clasp, but the third eye peeped out between the red wisps, dry and unblinking.

SERPENT

I found my silk scarf and got into bed with Marigold. We didn't bother to get up in the morning. I fixed us some cornflakes and toast about midday and then she huddled back down again while I drifted round the flat.

I drew for a bit. I tried to do a picture of Natasha on the back of the empty cornflake packet. I colored her and cut her out so that I could hold her in my hand. Then I stole a sheet of paper out of Star's school notebook and invented all these new outfits for Natasha. I drew big tags on the shoulders and cut them all out slowly, careful not to snip off a single tag. But the dresses and the coat and the frilly nightie didn't fit. The arms were in the wrong place so that Natasha's own pink cardboard arms waved about behind the empty

145

sleeves and even the necks weren't right, so the clothes hung stiffly at odd angles.

I realized I should have lain the cardboard Natasha down on paper and drawn round her to get an exact fit for the clothes but I was too disheartened to give it another go. I tried to pretend Natasha instead, inventing all sorts of games for us. Marigold must have heard me muttering because she came into the room rubbing her eyes.

"Is Star back?"

"No."

"She didn't say when she was coming?"

"No."

"It could be anytime, I suppose," said Marigold. "Micky might drive her back. And come up. Hey, we'd better get the place tidied up a bit, Dol. Oh God, I look such a sight—bath time! You come too. You look a bit grubby round the edges."

I loved sharing a bath with Marigold because her body looked so bright in the water, a living picture book to gaze at. I liked seeing all the tattoos that usually got covered up. There was a green and blue serpent that wiggled all the way down her spine, twisting first this way and then that, its long forked tongue flickering between her shoulder blades, the tip of its tail way down at the crease where her bottom began.

I traced the first few coils, and Marigold wriggled

her shoulders so that the serpent writhed convincingly. I'd never been all that sure about the serpent. It had tiny hooded eyes that looked sly and scary. Suddenly the serpent seemed too real, as if it were about to wriggle right off Marigold's back and slide up my own skin. I got out of the bath quick.

Marigold took ages. She was even longer getting dressed, trying on and discarding practically all her clothes. She ended up choosing an oldish pair of jeans and a pale pink T-shirt that belonged to Star. She wore pale pink lipstick too, and brushed her hair back behind her ears, which didn't suit her. If she hadn't had her vivid tattoos she'd have looked almost ordinary. I got it. She was trying to show Micky she wasn't crazy.

I didn't dare point out that Star had her train ticket back so Micky wouldn't be coming anywhere near our house. I didn't want Marigold to get mad at me again for being negative. And I was wrong. When Star came back at long last, not till the evening, she went straight to the window and waved. We heard the car start up and drive away.

Marigold dashed to the window too but Micky had gone.

"He drove you all the way from Brighton?" I mouthed.

"He wanted to make sure I was OK," said Star, showing off. "And that you were too."

"Of course we're OK," I said crossly.

Marigold was still pressed flat against the window. We both watched her anxiously. She looked as if she were going to step straight through it.

"Marigold?" said Star.

Her shoulders straightened. She turned, blinking hard, her eyes brimming. I could see the pulse flickering at her temple. She took a deep deep breath. Then she forced her pale pink lips into a silly smile.

"Did you have a good time, darling?" she asked.

"Yes, I did," said Star defiantly.

"Good. I'm so glad," said Marigold. "I think it's quite wonderful that you have this chance to know your father. Micky drove you all the way back? Why didn't you ask him up for a drink, sweetie?"

"He had to get back."

"Right," said Marigold. "Well. Did he say anything about seeing you again?"

"Next weekend," said Star.

"That's lovely," said Marigold, and she went to put her arms round Star.

Star stiffened at first but then she suddenly put her arms round Marigold's neck and hugged her hard.

"I did ask him to come in. And I told him how much you care about him. Oh, Marigold, I wish it could work out the way you want, you and him and Dol and me. I'm *sorry*. I felt so bad going. But I *had* to see him."

"Of course," said Marigold, cuddling her close. "He's your father. And he's wonderful, like I've always told you. You mustn't feel bad, my Starry girl, you must feel good. I expect Micky simply needed to have you all to himself this weekend. He needs this Sîan to act like a chaperone, right? I understand. Don't worry so. Dol and I had a lovely time together, didn't we, darling?"

"Yes. Yes we did. A lovely time," I repeated.

Star interrogated me privately when we went to bed.

"Shut up about it. A lot you care. If I'd told you on the phone she was chopping me up with a meat cleaver you still wouldn't have come back," I whispered bitterly.

"That's such a stupid thing to say! I was so worried. It kind of spoilt the whole weekend if you must know. I just kept phoning and phoning and wondering if you were all right."

"But you didn't come back early to see, did you?"

"Look, it's not like I'm your *mother*. It's not fair. Why should I always have to look after you?"

"Well, you don't. I can look after myself. I looked after Marigold too. She got all stroppy and weird but I handled it. I knew just what to do to get her sorted out."

"What do you mean, stroppy? What did she do?"

"Nothing. Because I stopped her."

"You're coming with me next Saturday."

"No I'm not."

"You are. You have to. You've got to get to know Micky."

"Why? He's not my father."

"I know he's not. But he's still going to look after you."

"What do you mean?"

"Dol. You have to keep this deadly secret. Do you swear?"

"Yes, OK. What is all this then?"

Star got out of her own bed and crept across to mine. She leant forward so that her breath tickled my face.

"I may be going to live with Micky," she whispered right in my ear.

"Live with him?"

"Shhh! Yes. And he says you can come too. We've discussed it all, him and me. And Sîan too. They don't always live together, she's got her own flat, but Micky's thinking of getting a bigger place for the four of us."

"And Marigold?"

"Don't be silly."

I thought about it, my head spinning. It was like one of the fairy tales. No, you don't have to stay locked up with the wicked witch. This handsome prince has come along and he's turned the two little beggar girls into princesses, even the scraggy ugly one, and they can all live in a new fairy castle together. Only Marigold wasn't a wicked witch. She was our mum.

"We can't leave her."

"We can still see her whenever we want. But Micky

says she should go into hospital for a bit. He says he knows this great place where they do all this therapy."

"She'd never go."

"If she'd just take this medicine—"

"But she wouldn't."

"Then that's not our fault. She's supposed to look after us. We're children. We're not supposed to look after her. The way I've always done. Well, I'm not doing it anymore. I've got two parents now. I want to be with my dad."

"I think you're horribly mean and selfish."

"What!" Star took hold of my shoulders and shook me hard. "How dare you! Look, I could have stayed with Micky today, that's what he wanted, it's what I wanted too, but I had to come back to get you all sorted out. I needn't have given you another thought, Dol, I could have just stayed with my dad, simple, perfect. But we kept thinking about you and how you maybe couldn't manage the way I have—"

"I *can* manage."

"And he's perfectly willing for you to come and live with us too. Don't you realize what a big thing that is? I mean, you're not his daughter and yet he's prepared to look after you, bring you up like he was your dad."

"I don't want him to be my dad. He doesn't care about me. He only cares about you."

"I'm his daughter."

"So you keep saying, over and over, until I'm sick of it."

"I'm sick of *you*, Dol. I thought you'd be thrilled."

"Well, I'm not. I don't want to live with him. I want to live with Marigold."

"OK then. If that's what you want," said Star. She got off my bed and climbed into her own.

We both lay still in the dark. I rubbed my scarf against my nose. I kept sniffing and swallowing. I hoped Star might think I was crying. I wanted her to feel mean. I wanted her to tell me she wouldn't go off to live with Micky without me. I wanted her to *stay*. I wanted to be the three of us, Marigold, Star and me, the way we'd always been.

Marigold was on her very best behavior all week. She didn't drink at all. She didn't shout or swear at anyone, she didn't go on a wild spending spree, she didn't stay in bed till lunchtime and stay up all night. She wore her mumsie jeans-and-T-shirt outfit and she made sure we had a proper tea every afternoon, baked beans on toast, sausage and chips, fish fingers, macaroni cheese.

"I think she heard you," I said to Star. "She's trying to make you want to stay."

"No. She's being all nicey-nicey because she wants to get round me. She wants me to tell her where Micky lives."

"Well, why *can't* she know?"

"He doesn't want to see her. He's got Sîan, I keep saying. He only stayed the other night because of me," said Star, tossing her head so that her hair fanned out. I wanted to grab two silky strands and tug hard.

"You think you're so special," I said bitterly.

"Micky thinks I'm special," said Star. "My dad. It's just magic between us."

"Yuck."

"You're just jealous."

"No, I'm not," I said, though I was so jealous I could hardly stand to speak to her.

"And Marigold is too. She keeps staring at me in this funny way, have you noticed?" said Star. "You know what makes me really mad? She can stop herself going crazy. She's been as sweet as sugar all week. She could control herself all the time if she really wanted and act like a normal mum."

"You always said she couldn't help it when she went funny."

"I know. I've always made excuses for her. I've done everything. When you were little and she went weird or got drunk I did everything for you. There's stuff she did that even you don't know about, Dol. I tried to look after you properly. I tried to look after *her*. And yet do you know something? It's never quite worked. It's never been enough. It's like she's this little girl at a party and you keep giving her presents but it's always the wrong ones."

"She liked her green clasp. She keeps wearing it."

"I don't mean literally. Oh, you're too young to understand."

I *felt* too young to understand. I wasn't sure if Star really meant all she was saying. She couldn't really seriously intend to leave forever next weekend. What about her precious school?

"I can go to any old school in Brighton," she said airily. "In fact Micky might even send me to a private school, he says I'd probably do even better then."

"What about all your friends?"

"I can make more friends."

"What about Mark?"

"Him!" said Star scornfully.

She meant it too. Micky must have given her lots of money because she took me to McDonald's one evening and bought me a cheeseburger and French fries, a strawberry milk shake and *two* ice cream sundaes with butterscotch sauce. Some of the boys hung round our table trying to talk to Star but she showed no interest in them whatsoever. I thought she was simply saving herself for Mark. He was larking about outside with his mates. Janice Taylor was there too.

"She's welcome to him," Star said to me.

When we went outside Mark called to her.

"Hey, Twinkle!"

She didn't even turn round.

"Twinkle little Star! Hey!" He bounded in front of her. "Where are you off to, then?"

"Home," said Star, pulling me along too.

"Come for a little walk first, eh?"

"No."

Mark stopped, obviously taken aback.

"What? Leave your little sister. Come on."

"No, I said. Are you deaf?" said Star.

"What's up with you?"

"I've just realized I don't have to hang around with guys like *you*," said Star.

She marched off so briskly I had to run to keep up. Mark missed a beat and then started yelling stuff after her. His mates joined in. They called Star awful names. I felt myself going red all over but Star stayed cool.

"You watch it, you pathetic creep. If my dad hears you calling me stuff like that he'll knock your yellow teeth right down your throat," she said.

"You're not going to be able to go back to McDonald's now," I said.

"I don't want to. Not with that crowd."

"I thought Mark was your boyfriend."

"No. Anyway, Micky doesn't think I'm anywhere near old enough for boyfriends," said Star, as if that settled it.

She didn't seem to care that *I* wouldn't be able to go back to McDonald's either.

"Don't you want a boyfriend now?" I asked.

"Not him. Hey, what about *your* boyfriend?"

"Who?"

"The owly one."

"Oliver."

"Ooh, Oliver, eh? Tell me all about him then."

"He's OK," I said, shrugging.

Oliver was more than OK. He'd had an unsettling weekend too. He was supposed to be going to Legoland with his dad and his dad's lady friend but his mum had had a migraine so he didn't go.

"I really badly wanted to go too, because it's meant to be pretty fantastic and I've always been nuts on Lego since I was a little kid. I designed my own Lego robots once and they had a war using these Lego laser guns and they kept zapping each other and collapsing and I'd be the robot repairman doing all this dramatic double-quick surgery to get them fit for battle again."

Some kid at the other end of the library sniggered. Oliver blinked behind his glasses.

"Of course that was when I was a very little kid," he said quickly.

"I play games like that sometimes, pretendy ones," I said. "So, will you get to go to Legoland next week?"

"I don't know. My dad was pretty narked with me. He said my mum was just putting it on and I should take no notice."

"*Was* she putting it on?"

Oliver fidgeted, twitching his nose so his glasses shot up and down.

"She does get lots of these migraines. She had to have a lie down on the couch. I have to keep the television turned right down so as not to disturb her."

"Well, at least you've got a television. Ours got taken away."

"She went to sleep. I could easily have gone to Legoland. Dolphin, does your mum get these migraines?"

"Not really. Well. She has a splitting headache if she's drunk too much the night before."

"Does your mum *drink*?" said Owly, his glasses going up and down like crazy. "What, lager and beer and stuff?"

"It's mostly vodka. It's only when she's . . . She gets these weird spells, see." I felt bad as soon as I'd said it. I put my hand to my mouth as if the words were blistering my lips. "Don't tell, Owly, will you?"

"*Oliver*. No, of course I won't." Oliver sighed. "Your mum sounds ever so exciting. Can I come to tea *soon*?"

"Well." I thought about it. Marigold was being so careful. But next week, if Star really went . . . I shook my head, trying to stop myself thinking about next week. It was far too scary.

Oliver mistook my head-shaking.

"Sorry. It's rude to keep on asking you."

"No, OK. Come tomorrow if you like. After school."

"Oh wow! Great! And I'll be able to see all her tattoos?"

"Not *all* of them, unless you creep up on her in her bath."

"Don't be silly," Oliver giggled, going pink. "And will she be drunk and fall over?"

"No! And she doesn't fall over anyway. Not even in her high heels."

"She wears wonderful clothes, your mum. It's like she's a rock star."

"You should see Star's dad then. He *really* looks like a rock star."

"I thought you didn't *have* a dad?"

"He's not mine. He's Star's. He and Marigold bumped into each other at an Emerald City concert."

"Go on!" Owly listened with his mouth open, as if I were telling him the latest plot in his favorite soap.

"Star thinks he's wonderful. She goes on and on about him. But I don't like him much. She keeps saying I'm jealous but I'm not. I don't want a dad."

"I don't want a dad either, not when he gets all huffy and cross," said Oliver. "But I did want to go to Legoland. It was my all-time second favorite destination."

"So OK, what's your first favorite?"

"Tea at your house, of course!"

I nudged him, making sure not to dig him too hard with my pointy elbow. He nudged me back, and then he got out his pencil case and unzipped his secret supply of mini white-chocolate bars.

"One for me and one for you," he said.

We slurped chocolate companionably.

"Hey hey hey, this is a library, not a canteen," said Mr. Harrison, bustling past. "At least have the decency to offer me a chunk, Arion and Dolphin, I have a secret passion for white chocolate."

"My name's Oliver, not Arion," said Oliver, giving Mr. Harrison his own bar.

"Golly gosh, a whole bar for me! You generous lad. I know perfectly well you're called Oliver. I was just making a posh literary allusion to amuse myself. There's this old legend where a guy called Arion plays sweet music on his harp and attracts this dolphin. Are you musical, Oliver?"

"I can nearly play 'We All Live in a Yellow Submarine' on the recorder."

"Hmm. Well, that's a start," said Mr. Harrison. He licked his lips. "Oh, yummy yummy. Please keep coming to my library, you two."

We didn't need any further encouragement. I was starting to look forward to my library lunchtimes with Oliver. The rest of the time at school still sucked, of course. I did try to swap seats in class so I could be next to Oliver. I talked this boy Brian into taking my place. Well, I had to bribe him a little, inking a Death by Harley skull and bike tattoo on his forearm. It's the tiredest tattoo in the book—millions of guys all over the world flash identical biceps—but Brian thought it dead original and seriously cool. Some of the other kids started clamoring for me to tattoo them too. I had quite a cluster round me when Miss Hill came into the classroom. I sat in Brian's seat and he ambled over to my old place next to Ronnie Churley. Everything seemed sorted. Ha. Miss Hill wasn't having it. She took roll call and then gave a double take.

"Go back to your original places at once, Brian and Dolphin."

"Oh, but Miss!"

"I am Miss *Hill*, Dolphin," she said, breathing out as she said it, as if she were blowing out birthday candles. "Now, I'm not having you playing Musical Chairs in my classroom whenever you feel like it. Sit back in your proper place, if you please."

"But—"

"Be quiet!" Miss Hill yelled.

Whenever she wanted silence she screamed. And then when it was silent she was the one who made the noise.

"Brian Barley! What is that black all over your arm?"

She didn't appreciate Brian's skin art. She sent him off to the cloakrooms to have a good scrub with soap.

"And I'm warning anyone else stupid enough to ink silly pictures all over themselves, I'm quite prepared to bring a bar of carbolic soap and a scrubbing brush to school and I'll scrub it off myself."

"Miss Hill would have a hard time scrubbing down old Bottle Nose! Look at her *neck*. It's almost as black as that stupid raggedy old dress she wears."

I felt my neck burning. I didn't know if they were just winding me up or if my neck really was black. It wasn't a place I ever saw. I tried to remember when I'd last washed it. And my dress wasn't raggedy, not now Star'd pinned the hem. It wasn't stupid. It was powerful. It was my witch dress.

I summoned up all my occult powers. I turned my head ever so casually and with just one wink of my witch's eyes I whisked Kayleigh and Yvonne right along the corridor and into the girls' toilets, where I stuck them down a loo each, headfirst, telling them to wash their own dirty necks.

Then I gazed at Miss Hill. I inked her all over, a full tattoo job: body, sleeve, every single wobbly little bit of her. I threw in a few piercings for good measure— studs along those arched eyebrows and a ring right through her snooty nose.

"Why are you staring at me, Dolphin?" she said,

highly irritated. "Get on with your work at once. You of all people need to practice your writing skills."

I tried to write. I could make up all sorts of stories, but the torrent of words in my head wouldn't slow down so I could copy them out on the page. The few that ended up on paper wiggled their letters round so that half of them were back to front.

Miss Hill ended up putting a big red line right across my page and told me to do it all over again. Oliver offered to help me at lunchtime in the library.

"You could tell me what you want to say. Then I could write it out for you and you could copy it," he suggested.

So we did that for a bit but it got boring and I sometimes mucked it up and copied the words all wrong.

"I'm not stupid, you know," I said fiercely, pushing the workbook away.

"I know," said Oliver. "You're dyslexic."

"Does that mean I just can't write properly?"

"That's it. You should have special help."

"I don't want to be special needs. Yeah, dyslexic—that's what they called me at my last school but one. How do you spell it then?"

"Don't ask me. It's a daft word for people who can't write properly. I'm top in spelling and yet I haven't got a clue."

"You're top in everything, Mr. Smarty Pants."

"You should be top in drawing. That was a *great* tattoo you did for Brian. You don't do your mum's, do you?"

"No, of course not! You have to do, like, an apprenticeship, and there's heaps of stuff to learn, and you have to be seriously scrupulous about sterilizing. But I can draw on skin OK. I'll do you, if you like."

"After school, eh? When I'm at your place."

"You're scared Miss Hill will get you into trouble, right? Well, under that boring old beige blouse and navy skirt *she's* a Technicolor dream, I kid you not." I turned over my page and started drawing a naked tattooed Miss Hill.

"Oh, Dolphin, your story's on the other side! You won't be able to hand it in now," Oliver said, sighing, but he spluttered when he saw what I was drawing.

"Wow. It really *looks* like her. Oh, look what you're doing on her chest! Little faces, and their mouths are . . . oh!" Oliver's glasses started to steam up in his excitement.

I was getting inspired. I drew the wildest and lewdest and most imaginative tattoos ever, making full use of all her body parts.

"You are dreadful!" said Oliver. "I'll never be able to look at Miss Hill again."

At that exact moment Miss Hill walked into the library!

Oliver gasped. I whizzed my drawing off the table and into my lap in double-quick time.

"Hello, Mr. Harrison. I've come to collect those books for the Victorian project," said Miss Hill. She looked over at us. "Whatever is the matter, Oliver?"

Oliver's mouth stayed helplessly open. I could see his eyes revolving behind his glasses.

"Oliver's worried because he was helping me with my story, Miss. Miss *Hill*. And he was worried it would get him into trouble, but I said you'd be pleased that he was helping me. It's very kind of him, isn't it, Miss Hill?"

"Well. Yes. Although really you should do the work yourself, Dolphin. Is that your story you're clutching in your lap? Let me see how far you've got."

Oliver gave an agonized gasp.

"No, this is just a first attempt and I mucked it up," I said, crumpling it quickly into my palm. "But I'm about to try again, aren't I, Oliver?"

Oliver nodded, incapable of speech.

"Very well. I shall await this story with bated breath," said Miss Hill, bustling over to the Victorian section.

Mr. Harrison went with her. When she'd squeaked off across the polished floor right out the door he turned and winked at us.

"I don't know what is actually *on* that scrap of paper in your hand, Dolphin, but I should hide it right away."

164

"Very good advice, Mr. Harrison," I said, sticking it in my pocket.

"P-h-e-w!" said Oliver, wiping his brow under his long floppy bangs.

"Pull yourself together now, Oliver. Old Tattoo-Tummy is going to make a real point of asking for my story now," I said.

Oliver collapsed into helpless giggles.

"Shhh now!" said Mr. Harrison. "Settle down. Stop being wicked, Dolphin."

I shushed, I settled, I stopped. I liked Mr. Harrison so much I'd have done anything for him. I wished like anything he could be my teacher but he had the Year Threes and I'd missed being one of them. They all loved him. Whenever he was on playground duty they clustered round him and hung on his hand, like he was their dad. I wished he were *my* dad.

I wrote a story called MY DAD. Well, I told Oliver and he wrote it and I copied it. My hand was *aching* by the time I got to the end of it.

MY DAD

I have this really super dad who can only come and see me once or twice a year because he is always making trips across all the seas in the world observing dolphins. That is why I am called Dolphin. My dad can understand dolphin squeaks and he can swim amongst all the dolphins and next time he

*comes to get me he's going to let me go off with him
and I will get to ride on a dolphin's back and I bet
everyone will envy me and my best friend Oliver
might get to have a ride on a dolphin too.*

"Really?" said Oliver.

"Really ride on a dolphin?" I said. "Well, not *really*
really."

"No, really am I your best friend?"

"Yes. You're coming to tea, aren't you?" I said.

I was starting to get worried about it. We met up
with Star after school and she was unusually sweet,
chatting away to Oliver as if he were her special little
brother, telling him this long funny story about some
silly mishap with her hockey stick. Oliver kept giggling. I hung back a step, starting to feel left out, but he
lagged a little too, keeping time with me.

Star nipped inside the newsagent's for a moment
and he said shyly, "I like your sister."

"Yes. Everyone does. She's ever so pretty, isn't she?
Her *hair*!"

"It's lovely." Oliver paused. "But not as nice as yours."

This was such a sweet but stupid comment that I
went bright red.

"What's up with you, Dol?" said Star, coming out
of the shop with a big paper bag.

"Nothing."

"What have you been saying to make her blush, Oliver?"

"Nothing."

"You're like a pair of little parrots, nothing nothing nothing," said Star. "Here, help yourselves."

She offered us the paper bag. She'd bought sherbet saucers, banana toffee chews, fizzy cola bottles, liquorice wheels and long red jelly snakes.

"Yummy yummy!" said Oliver.

We sucked and licked happily all the way home. I felt a bit sick as we went through the broken garden gate and up the path to the front door. The sweet stickiness in my mouth went all metallic.

"You live in quite a big house," said Oliver politely. "Ours is just a semi, and we might have to move into a flat soon."

"Ours is a flat. There's an old boot who lives downstairs. We live on the middle floor. And there's a ghost upstairs."

"A ghost?" said Oliver, giggling expectantly.

"Not a silly spook in a white nightie. A real awful moldering maggotty ghost with bits falling off him at every step."

Oliver blinked and stood still.

"Shut up," said Star, putting her key in the door. "Take no notice, Oliver. It's just the man upstairs died and no one's come to clear away his things yet and once Dol and me thought we could still hear him shambling around upstairs."

"Really?" said Oliver.

"Not *really* really," I said. "You can never suss out what's real and what's not, Oliver!"

I followed Star through the door and pulled Oliver after me. I could smell baking even from downstairs. I exchanged glances with Star. She looked tense too, wondering if Marigold had baked a hundred and one cakes again, but when we got upstairs we found it was just *one* cake, a special iced sponge with a big brown marzipan owl on top.

"It's specially for you, Owly," said Marigold.

"Oh, Marigold, he's *Oliver*, not Owly," I said.

But Oliver didn't seem to mind.

"Thank you," he whispered, admiring the cake. He kept darting little glances at Marigold, admiring her too, though I could tell he was disappointed that there wasn't much of her on display. She was wearing jeans and a long-sleeved shirt with the collar turned up so her third eye was hidden.

"It's not *just* cake for tea, is it, Marigold?" said Star.

"Of course not, sweetie. There's sausage and beans and chips. And fruity yogurt. And real fruit too, apples and bananas and mandarin oranges." Marigold recited this menu anxiously, waiting for our approval.

We ate it all. Oliver got the slice of cake with the owl. Then we finished up the rest of Star's sweets.

"I thought you said you didn't get much to eat at home," Oliver whispered. "I've had *heaps*." He idly sucked at his red jelly snake as he helped clear the table.

"You don't have to do that, sweetheart," said Marigold, dodging backward and forward to the kitchen, still practicing being a normal mother.

"I don't mind a bit. I like to help. Thank you for the *lovely* tea," said Oliver a little indistinctly, because he'd wedged his snake between his teeth so he could have both hands free for the dishes.

"You're a young man after my own heart," said Marigold, rolling up her sleeves to wash the dishes.

She saw Oliver staring at her arms and pulled her sleeves down again quickly.

"Oliver likes your tattoos," I said. "Show him my dolphin."

Marigold seemed hesitant. She glanced over her shoulder. Star had gone into our bedroom, saying she had to get on with her homework.

"OK," said Marigold, and let Oliver see the dolphin tattoo.

"C-o-o-l!" breathed Oliver, the glistening red tail of his snake hanging out of his mouth.

"Show him *your* snake, Marigold," I said.

Marigold glanced over her shoulder again, double-checking Star was nowhere around. Then she pulled the tail of her shirt right up under her armpits and showed Oliver the long green coils of her serpent.

"Ooooh!" said Oliver.

Marigold swayed gently to and fro so that the serpent slid sinuously up and down her spine.

"Ooooh!" said Oliver, and his mouth opened so wide his own snake dropped out of his mouth, slithered down his T-shirt and ended up stuck on his bare pink leg.

"My tattoo," said Oliver. "Oh, I can't wait till I'm grown up. I want to have tattoos all over."

"Run and get your felt-tips, Dol," said Marigold. "Right, Oliver! Your wish is our command."

We sat Oliver on the sofa between us. Marigold drew serpents and dragons and dinosaurs up and down his left arm while I drew unicorns and mermaids and stars all over his right. Oliver looked left and right, right and left, as if he were watching tennis. His smile stretched from ear to ear.

Star came out the bedroom once to go to the bathroom. Marigold started nervously. Star just shook her head and said, "Gross."

"Do I look gross?" Oliver asked, sounding enormously pleased.

He nearly cried when it was time for him to go home and we had to scrub his tattoos away.

"No, *please*, I want to keep them!" he begged, though he admitted his mum would be shocked.

"Then she might not let you come round to my place again, Oliver," I said.

"OK then. Because I *so* want to come again. This has been my best day ever."

Star and I walked him home. He burbled happily until he got near his house. His mother was watching for him behind the curtains. His house looked alarmingly tidy. Even the flowers in the garden looked like soldiers on parade. It was my turn to go to tea with Oliver next but I wasn't at all sure it was going to be enjoyable.

When Star and I got back home we caught Marigold having a drink, and she kept going out to the kitchen for another sly swig, though she wasn't fooling anyone.

"Little Owly really enjoyed himself," she said.

"*Oliver*. But yes, he did," I said. "Thanks for being so nice to him, Marigold. He thinks you're wonderful."

"Does he?" said Marigold, looking to see if Star was listening. She stretched out on the sofa, pretending to be relaxed. "Saturday tomorrow," she said. She paused. Star didn't react. She was staring into space.

"What are your plans, Star, sweetheart?" Marigold asked.

Star smoothed back her hair, licked her lips, pressed her knees together.

"I'm going to Brighton."

"I thought so," said Marigold. "You've been in touch with Micky, then?"

"Yep."

"Great," said Marigold. "That's just great."

She heaved herself off the sofa and went to the kitchen. We heard the clank of the bottle on the rim of her glass. Then she came back, the glass brimming.

"Marigold. Don't!" I said huskily.

"What? It's water, darling," said Marigold, taking several gulps. "So, Star. It looks as if it's going to be a lovely sunny day. Dolly and I might very well come too. To Brighton." She drank again.

"Don't," Star said. Gently.

"We'll go with you, darling. The three of us. And we'll meet up with Micky."

"No," said Star.

"Yes," said Marigold. "We're coming too and you can't stop us."

Star didn't even bother to reply. She just looked at Marigold in a pitying way.

"Don't look at me like that," said Marigold. "I don't know why you're always looking down on me. I've tried so hard, I've done my best, I want to be a good mother—"

"You are a good mother. You're the best in the world," I said, going to her and taking her glass away so that I could give her a hug.

"S-Star?" said Marigold, her voice slurring.

Star came slowly over to the sofa. She sat down beside Marigold and put her arm round her. She cuddled her and I cuddled in too and we stayed like that for a long time. But we were all so tense it didn't feel like a proper cuddle at all. It felt stiff instead of soft, as if we were stone statues. Then Marigold leant more heavily and started breathing deeply. She'd gone to sleep. Star slid away from her and went into the bedroom.

I eased a pillow under Marigold's head, covered her up with a blanket and followed Star.

She had her schoolbag and two carrier bags packed up, ready.

"You're really not coming back!" I said, and I burst into tears.

"Don't, Dol. Please. I can't bear it," said Star, crying too.

"Don't go."

"I *have* to. You can still come with me."

"No I can't."

"Well. See what happens. I'll leave the mobile here and phone you every day to make sure you're all right. Anytime you want to come just say."

"Let me have Micky's number."

"I can't."

"I won't tell Marigold."

"You might not mean to. But she'd get it out of you."

"How are you going to stop her tagging along tomorrow?"

"That's easy enough," said Star.

173

And it was. Star got into my bed and held me close until I eventually went to sleep. I woke up around six but she was already gone.

I waited for Marigold to wake up. I hoped she'd sleep half the morning. But she woke early too, in spite of her hangover.

"It's a lovely sunny morning, my girls," she said, coming into our room.

She was knuckling her forehead, trying to ease a headache. Then she saw Star's empty bed and stopped dead, her arm still raised. She didn't say anything. She just lay down on Star's bed and started crying. These were new horrible heartbroken tears, as if she were choking. It sounded as if her serpent had coiled itself right round her neck.

BATS

I thought Marigold might rush us down to Brighton again but she seemed to have given up on that idea. Her headache was bad and the crying made it worse so she went back to her own bed. I didn't know what to do. I didn't want to play in my own bedroom because it seemed so empty without Star. *I* felt empty, totally hollow, as if all my insides had been sucked out of me. I wandered round and round the living room, feeling so eerily light that I felt I'd be bobbing up to the ceiling any minute. Then I thought of Mr. Rowling stumbling about on his moldering feet directly above my head. I looked up at the grimy ceiling. It was easy to imagine the stains of grisly footprints. It got so I couldn't stand it so I woke Marigold, even though I knew she'd probably be bad-tempered.

She was mean at first. She'd got it into her head that I'd ganged up with Star and knew all about her slipping off early. This was so unfair that I started crying. Then she cried too, and we had a cuddle. She smelt bad from the drink but I didn't mind too much.

"My Dol," she said, all safe and sweet again. "Sorry I was horrid to you, darling. I'll make it up to you, I promise. We'll have a lovely weekend, just you and me. And then Star will come home and we'll be us three girls again. That's what's the matter, isn't it? We're just missing her."

I cried harder. I didn't know what Marigold would do when she found out Star was gone for good. I didn't know how I was going to cope. I felt emptier than ever, a balloon girl with a trailing string lost in the emptiness of the sky. I clung to Marigold and she rocked me. I mumbled something about feeling empty. Marigold thought I meant I was hungry.

"I'm hungry too. Starving. We'll go out for lunch, right, and then we'll do a big big shop. Yes, we'll buy lots of goodies. We'll make sure there's a special tea for Star when she comes back—and just in case Micky comes in with her we'll get some beer in for him. We could make it like a little party. . . ."

She was off again. There was no way I could stop her. She wanted to take me to McDonald's and I couldn't stop that either—"Don't be so silly, Dolly, you *love* McDonald's'—but to my great relief there was no sign of Mark and his mates, it was just crowded out with mums and kids.

Marigold hardly ate anything herself even though she said she was starving. She bought lots for me, even selecting two butterscotch sundaes just the way Star had done. It made me miss Star terribly.

Did she really really mean it? Wasn't she ever going to come back? How could she leave Marigold? How could she leave me?

My tummy went tight. Sour ice cream suddenly hurtled backward from my stomach and I had to dash to the toilets. I felt emptier than ever afterward.

Marigold took me on the promised shopping spree, using the credit card I was so worried about. We bought food, we bought drink—too much drink—and we bought clothes, new black jeans and a long-sleeved black satin shirt for Marigold, new blue jeans and blue shirts for Star and me. New nighties too, black lace for Marigold, blue and white gingham check with white lace trim for Star and me. Marigold even bought blue and white paint to brighten up our bedroom, though I tried to stop her.

She was tired when we got home and she had a drink or two. Then the phone rang. I only got to talk to Star for two seconds because Marigold grabbed the phone from me. She tried so hard to sound sweet and mumsie and normal that the veins stood out on her white forehead.

"You're having a lovely time, darling? Good! Hey, bad girl, you shouldn't have left early like that. Slipping off to the station yourself! I don't know. But Micky met you OK? Can I have a little word with him, sugar bunch? I just want to check how things are, see what time you're both coming back. Hey, we're going to have a little party for you. You'll make sure Micky comes, right? Star? *Star?*"

She drank quite a lot after Star rang off. I didn't mind quite so much because she'd bought me one more present, new felt-tips and a big drawing book. I drew me in my witch's black velvet, with a special silver glitter outline all round me to make me extra powerful and totally protected. Then I drew me walking along and exercising my witchly powers on anyone who got on my nerves. I redrew Miss Hill, tattooing her even more inventively. It started to look a bit like a comic strip. I decided to show it to Oliver in the library on Monday. I could maybe draw speech bubbles and tell him what to put and then he could write the words in for me.

I drew Oliver but this time my witchly powers waxed white instead of black and he grew taller and tougher and his eyes became laser-powerful, so they could sizzle straight through his specs, searing everyone in sight. I gave him a haircut too, snipping off his long lank bangs and wispy strands until he just had a butch bristle left, transforming his face.

I drew Star and I gave her a haircut too. I gave her a terrible unflattering bob that left her neck long and awkward and her face too exposed. I dotted spots all over her skin and bloated her body so that she was so fat she bulged right out of her clothes. She waddled desperately after a stick-man Micky. He was running hard from this horror of a daughter. I drew tears and snot dribbling down Star's face—but her expression looked too real. I suddenly felt frightened. I tore the page out and shredded it into little pieces.

I started to draw Star again but I didn't trust my pen. I tried Marigold instead, but I was too tired, and I couldn't be bothered to ink in all her tattoos. She looked really odd without them, the way most people look in their underwear.

"Look, Marigold," I said.

She was asleep, her head on the table.

"That's beautiful, Dol darling," she whispered, and then I went to bed.

Marigold was up before me the next morning. She woke me with a breakfast tray. I blinked at it in astonishment. I stared at Marigold. She'd tied her hair up in an old chiffon scarf and was wearing an old shirt and a pair of knickers.

"Come on, sleepyhead, eat up," said Marigold. "You need a big breakfast. We've got work to do."

"Work?"

"Yes, work, Dolly Daydream. Why do you think we bought the paint yesterday? We're going to transform your bedroom. Star doesn't like all the stars and stuff, she thinks it's childish. She wants a pretty, conventional bedroom."

"I like the stars," I said, fidgeting anxiously. "And all the dolphins."

My orange juice tipped and spread a gaudy stain across the sheets.

"Clumsy," said Marigold, but she wasn't cross. "Still, it's time they had a good wash." She was already getting to work scrubbing down the walls.

"Please, Marigold. I want it to stay the way it is. It's my bedroom too."

"Oh, darling, we're going to make it so much prettier. Star will love it. Blue—such a beautiful blue—with a white gloss surround. It'll be such a surprise for her. If we really get cracking it'll all be done when she gets back."

"What if . . ." I couldn't finish it.

I tried to eat my cornflakes, spooning in several mouthfuls. The mush stayed in my mouth. I pushed it in one cheek and then the other. It wouldn't go down. I gave up and spat it back into the bowl when Marigold wasn't watching.

I helped her all day long, scrubbing down, covering up all our clutter with old sheets and newspapers, and then painting. I was scared she'd see some of Star's stuff was gone but she didn't notice. Star hadn't taken much, just her favorite jeans, her boots with heels, her sneakers, her best skirt, several tops, her jacket, a couple of books, her hairbrush, her nail varnish, and her new teddy bear. Maybe she didn't mean it. She'd come back this evening.

But she didn't. Marigold started to get the tea ready as soon as she'd finished painting. She hummed as she arranged little tidbits prettily on plates. She was still in her shirt and knickers, dancing around to Emerald City, playing the fool. She saw me staring at her.

"What? OK, OK, I'd better get some proper clothes on. Before they come." She frowned. "Why are you looking at me like that, Dol?" She peered down at herself. "Do I look awful? I don't look all old and scraggy, do I?"

"No, of course not. You look young. And pretty."

"Pretty awful, do you mean?" Marigold looked down at herself anxiously. She peered at her long thighs. A flock of bats flew upward, their wings outstretched, the largest no bigger than my thumbnail, the smallest not much more than a black dot. "I got such dreadful stretch marks when I was expecting you. I got so sick and fat, yet with Star I hardly showed right up until the end. *Look* at these marks!" Her long nails

181

scrabbled at them as if she could scratch them straight off her skin. "Maybe if I had a cover-up tattoo over the bats? But it upsets Star so."

"Star Star Star," I said. "Why do you have to keep going on about her all the time?"

"Oh, Dol, don't be so silly," Marigold said, pulling her jeans on and covering up her legs. "Does this shirt look OK? There's little painty spots but that maybe makes it look homey?"

"You love Star more than you love me," I said.

"I love you both," said Marigold. She hesitated. "But Star is Micky's child."

"Yes, and she's with him now," I said. "She's gone to him. I've stayed with you. Why can't you love *me* best?"

"Don't start a stupid scene, Dol," Marigold said briskly, stepping into her high strappy sandals. "Star and Micky could come back any minute. Now stop the nonsense and help me get everthing ready."

I went and sat on my bed in the newly painted bedroom. All the stars were lost under a blur of blue. I cried.

"Cheer up, silly crybaby," said Marigold.

But as the hours went by Marigold grew shrill.

"Where *are* they? What's happened? Oh God, you don't think there's been a crash, do you?"

The phone suddenly rang, startling her so that her

arms flew up in the air. I reached for it but she was there first.

"Star, darling! Oh, thank God! You're all right? And Micky? Why are you so *late*? Where are you? What? What did you say? I don't understand. What do you mean? You're still in Brighton? But you're not going to be back till late. *What?* You're not making sense, sweetie. You're not going to be back? What do you *mean*?"

Marigold babbled on and on into the phone, clutching it so tight she embedded it into her head.

"What do you *mean*?" she repeated again and again.

Then her whole stance changed as if an electric shock had gone through her.

"Micky! Look darling, what is Star *on* about? Why are you still in Brighton? It's going to take you *hours* to get here. No. *No!* Look, she's not staying with you. Not even overnight. For God's sake, put her in the car and come here. We can talk it over then. She can't stay. She hasn't got any of her *things*. What? Look, there's school. She can't miss school. Wait till the summer holidays, it's not long now. Then she can stay a few days, that's a lovely idea. But she can't stay now. I won't allow it. I'm her mother. Micky. Micky, please."

She bent right over, tears spilling down her face.

"Star," she whispered. "Please, Star. Come home. Don't do this to me. Look, we've got a surprise for you,

Dol and me. What? No, Star, I'm talking to you—oh, *please . . ."*

She shook her head but then held the phone out to me. Its imprint was marked clearly on her face, a crude new tattoo.

I took the phone from her. Star was crying on the other end.

"Dolly? Are you all right?"

"Yes. No. Oh, Star, please, come home. I can't manage without you."

"I can't come. Don't make me feel even worse. I'm sorry, Dol, I'm so sorry. Look, I'll phone every day. I'll keep in touch. You'll be OK. *I* had to cope with her right from when I was little, I looked after her *and* you. You said yourself she's better with you. I think I just made it harder for her because I'm Micky's. Look, I won't stay away forever. I'll come back soon, I promise, but I just have to stay now. I *have* to be with him. He's my dad. This is my one chance to be with him. If I come back now she'll never let go of me, you know that. Oh, Dol, I feel so bad, but you do understand, don't you?"

"No, I don't! Star! Come back. You can't leave me!"

"I have to," said Star, and the phone went dead.

I let it drop out of my sticky hand.

"No! Don't! Give it to me!" Marigold cried, on her hands and knees, grabbing for it.

She started yelling into it, screaming at Star.

"She's hung up. She's not there. Stop it! She's left

us, she's left us forever. I hate her, I hate her, I hope she never comes back," I shouted.

I clawed the phone away from Marigold and bashed it hard against the wall, again and again.

"You'll break it!" Marigold screamed.

I stopped dead. I shook the phone. I tried to dial a number. It was no use. It was broken.

"We'll get another," I said quickly. "You can get one on that credit card."

Marigold shook her head. "She can't ring on any other phone. She won't know the number. And we don't know hers."

"Oh! Oh, Marigold," My legs buckled and I slid to the floor.

She reached out. I ducked, thinking she was going to hit me, but she just wiped my tears with her fingers.

"I didn't mean to!" I sobbed.

"I know. It's all right. It's not your fault. Did you know Star was going for good?"

"I'm sorry," I wept.

"Never mind," said Marigold. "Never mind, never mind."

She said it over and over again until the words lost all sense. Then she started drinking. I stayed with her for a while and then sloped off into the bedroom. It still smelt terribly of paint. I couldn't shut the white gloss door because it was still sticky.

I got into bed but I couldn't sleep. I wanted Star so

badly I got into her bed to sniff the faint talcumy smell of her still on her pillow. But it made me angry too. I punched the pillow, harder and harder. Then I missed and punched the wall instead. It hurt so much that I huddled into a ball, tucking my fist into my armpit.

I was acting like the crazy person now, smashing everything. Maybe I was going to go mad like Marigold. We'd both end up in the loony bin. While Star had her shiny new life with her father.

I couldn't wake Marigold in the morning. She'd managed to get herself to bed but the vodka bottle was empty. I stood shivering, staring at her. She was breathing heavily, her eyes open a fraction. I shook her hard. She mumbled a bit but she didn't make sense.

I got myself ready for school, creeping round the flat. I backed away from the broken phone on the floor as if it could bite me. I grabbed a handful of the stale party snacks left out all night and then went out the door. I tiptoed down the stairs but Mrs. Luft was out like a flash.

"You! That row last night! Screaming, shouting, bang bang banging. I'm going to get you all evicted, you see if I don't. Where's your sister?"

"It's none of your business," I said, and I ran out of the house.

It was so odd walking down the road without Star. It felt as if a part of *me* was missing. When I turned the corner there was Ronnie Churley right in front of me. I stopped dead, but he was with his mum, not his mates. All he could do was stick his tongue out at me when she wasn't watching. He looked a bit embarrassed, Mr. Tough Guy discovered trotting along with Mummy.

I stuck my tongue out back at him and then skipped past, singing out, "Mummy's little diddums."

He'd get me for it later, but it was worth it. I was on my own. It was cool to walk alone to school.

Ronnie Churley's mum looked horrible too, a frowny lady with those funny trousers with little straps that go under the foot to stop them wrinkling. She needed a strap under her chin and all to straighten out her face wrinkles.

I didn't think much of any of their mums. Not even Tasha's. Marigold was much younger and much prettier. Oliver thought so too.

He was already in the playground, leaning against the railings right at the front. He often hung about there because it was so public it was hard for anyone to pick on him.

"Hi, Dolphin!" He waved at me frantically. He was so short-sighted he always thought no one else could see a foot in front of their face.

"Hi," I said, climbing up over the railing and swinging down the other side instead of bothering to go all the way round to the front entrance. The hem of my witch skirt caught. I unhooked it, seeing tiny toads and black cats and bats fluttering free.

A flock of bats whirled round my head so that I could barely see.

"Dolphin? What is it? Have you hurt yourself?" said Oliver.

"It's not me. It's my mum," I said, and I started crying.

"Don't!" said Oliver. "Oh, Dolphin, don't, please. Don't cry."

He put his skinny arm awkwardly round my neck. There was a shriek from the other side of the railings.

"Look at Bottle Nose and Owly! They're practically snogging. Yuck!"

"Quick. Come round the back of the playground toilets," said Oliver urgently.

There was a narrow gap between the girls' building and the boys'. Oliver edged into the middle and pulled me after him. I stood bolt upright beside him, tears still trickling down my face.

"Haven't you got a paper hankie?" said Oliver.

"No, I haven't," I said, scrubbing at my eyes with the back of my hand. I gave a big sniff. "Stop staring at me."

"It's all right. I cry too. I cried this weekend because my mum cried when Dad brought me back."

"Well, I haven't got a dad. Star has. And she's gone

off with him and now I've broken the phone and we can't get in touch and Marigold . . . She's drinking. She wouldn't even wake up this morning. You don't know what it can be like. Star always did stuff, cleaned her up and looked after her when she was really bad. I don't know how to do it. I don't know how to do anything without Star. She's not just like my sister. She's like my mum too. And my best friend. And now she's walked out on me and I haven't got anyone."

I started sobbing again.

"You've got me," said Oliver.

We could hear the bell ringing in the playground.

"We'd better go," I said. "We can't really hole up here all day long."

"I mean it, Dolphin. I can be your best friend. I'd like that," said Oliver, and he twisted his head round and kissed my cheek, even though it was all teary and disgusting.

Then he edged out quick. It took me several seconds to squeeze out after him, but he was still bright red, with his glasses all steamed up. He looked incredibly silly but I managed to give him a wobbly smile.

"OK, best friend. Lessons. And then let's make up our own comic strip in the library at lunch."

"Oh wow, yes, let's."

"And—and maybe Star will be back by tonight."

"Yes, I bet she'll come back right away," said Oliver.

I counted in sevens and made endless wishes and bargains and made up witchy spells all day long. As I ran home I touched each lamppost and whispered "Star" seven times over for every one so that she would be waiting for me in our new blue and white bedroom.

She wasn't waiting. Marigold was lying on her bed, still in her nightdress. She didn't get up all afternoon and evening, apart from stumbling to the toilet like a zombie.

"Why don't you clean your teeth and have a wash?" I suggested.

"Teeth? Wash?" Marigold repeated, as if I were speaking a foreign language. "What's the point?"

"Well. It'll make you feel better."

She took no notice and got another bottle from the cupboard.

"Don't drink. Eat," I said, and I made us both some tea.

Marigold said she didn't want any. I tried to prop her up against her pillow and help her sip a cup of tea but half of it dribbled down her chin.

"Please try, Marigold," I begged.

"I don't want to try," she said. "Just let me be." She slid back down under her duvet.

I watched over her for a while. She seemed to be asleep. I wasn't sure if she was drunk or not. I fidgeted around her, staring at her closed eyes and tousled hair and Technicolor skin.

I vaguely heard a faint ringing from downstairs. And then a minute later there was a banging at the door.

"You in there! Come and answer this door."

It was Mrs. Luft. I decided to take no notice but she went on banging.

"Oh God, my head," Marigold groaned, going further under the duvet. "Get rid of the old bag, Dol."

"I don't like her. She's horrid to me. *You* go," I said.

I had as much chance of the duvet rising upward and slithering to the door to deal with Mrs. Luft. I had to go myself.

"For goodness' sake, about time!" Mrs. Luft shouted when I opened our door an inch. "What's going *on* in there?"

"Nothing, nothing," I said. I opened the door properly, stepped outside and pulled it to behind me. I couldn't have her barging in and seeing Marigold in a stupor.

"This is a one-off. I want to make that crystal clear. It's a total liberty. I've got better things to do than climb up all these stairs. You don't even answer the door straightaway like normal folk. Anyway, it's tying up my phone. Someone might be wanting to speak to *me*."

I suddenly understood.

"My sister! She's phoned you!" I started flying down the stairs.

"Hey, hey! Wait for me. Don't you dare go in my flat by yourself, young lady! The cheek of it!"

I had to hover until she got there herself and then trail after her into her darkly polished domain. She made me wipe my feet on her doormat. She'd probably douse the telephone with disinfectant the minute I'd stopped using it.

"Star?"

"Oh, Dol. Oh, Dol. Oh, Dol." Star was crying. "What's happened? What's the matter with the mobile phone? I was so worried when I couldn't get through. And then I suddenly thought of Mrs. Luft. What's Marigold done? Has she smashed the phone? She hasn't done anything to you, has she?"

I thought quickly, my eyes swiveling round Mrs. Luft's horrible brown living room. She had a mottled browny-pink lamp and a matching vase that looked like liver sausage. I put out my hand to touch the vase to see if it felt like liver sausage too. Mrs. Luft flicked my fingers away, outraged.

"Dol! Tell me. What's *happened*?"

"It's been so awful," I said. I turned my back on Mrs. Luft and started whispering. "She's been so drunk."

"Well. She often is," said Star.

"No. Worse. So violent. She broke the phone. She . . . she hit me and hit me. I'm bleeding. I think she's broken something," I whispered. "And now . . . now she's drunk an entire bottle, no, two, and she's in a coma and . . . and she might even be *dead*."

"Oh, Dol! It's all right. I'll come and—"

But a whirlwind in a nightdress barged uninvited into Mrs. Luft's flat and snatched the telephone before I could stop her.

"Star? Oh, Star, sweetie, how brilliant of you to phone Mrs. Luft," said Marigold, without so much as a slur to her voice.

"It was dreadful cheek and it's certainly not going to happen ever again!" said Mrs. Luft. "Now get off that phone!"

"In a minute," Marigold muttered, obviously trying to concentrate on what Star was saying. "I did *what*, Star, sweetie? No, it was Dolly, but it was an accident. We'll get another phone. But why don't you and Micky stop playing silly games and give me *his* phone number? No, of course I'm not drunk, darling. Do I sound drunk? *What?* OK, speak to Dol again, but we've got to talk too."

"Not on *my* phone you don't!" said Mrs. Luft indignantly. "Just say your goodbyes. I can't believe you can be so rude."

Marigold pressed the phone into my palm. I didn't hold it too close to my ear. Star's words shot out like bullets.

"Dol? How *could* you lie like that? She's not in a coma, she's not even drunk. I was so *scared*! How could you say it?"

"She did, she did," I mumbled, though Marigold was standing right in front of me, staring into my face.

"You were just lying to get me to come home. So it was *you* who broke the phone?"

"No. Yes. Look, Star, please, please come back now—"

"Why should I? It's not *fair*. I want to do what *I* want just this once. Now listen. We'll send you another phone, right? But don't you dare ever tell lies like that again."

"Star—"

"No. I'm putting the phone down now."

"Please!"

I heard a click and then the purr of the freed line.

"Let me talk now," said Marigold.

"No, this has gone too far. Put my phone down at once," said Mrs. Luft.

Marigold snatched the phone from me and then heard the dialing tone herself.

"Put it *down!*" Mrs. Luft commanded.

Marigold did as she was told, her hand trembling so that she could barely slot the receiver back into its socket.

"Thank you very much," said Mrs. Luft sarcastically. "Now if it's not too much trouble could you both go back upstairs to your own place? And don't you *dare* use my flat as your personal telephone box. Get your own phone reconnected and stop wasting all your money on your disgusting habits. Look at you, wandering round in your skimpy nightie, showing off all your lurid tattoos. What sort of example are you to your little girls? No wonder one seems to have scarpered. Who would want a mother like you?"

I expected Marigold to yell a whole load of abuse. But she didn't say a word. Her eyes looked dazed. She turned and picked her way toward the door in her bare feet.

"Look at those black soles! You'll make marks all over the carpet," said Mrs. Luft.

Marigold didn't seem to be listening.

"*I* want my mum. She's the best mum in the whole world," I said.

"What rubbish. I heard what you were saying, how she hits you. When the pair of you have been screaming I've had it in mind to phone the welfare people."

"You mustn't! Please don't. There's nothing wrong. Marigold's never hit me, ever ever ever," I said. "Don't tell anyone, please."

Mrs. Luft folded her arms triumphantly.

"We'll have to see, won't we?" she said. "Look, it's for your own good."

"Marigold! Tell her. Tell her you've never done anything to me. I made up some stuff but I didn't mean it. *Marigold!*"

Marigold was already halfway upstairs so I ran after her. I pulled at her arm.

195

"Marigold, we have to tell her everything's fine. We can't have her phoning any welfare people, can we?"

"Why not?" Marigold said, her voice sounding flat and far away.

"Because they might put me in a home!"

"Maybe you'd be better off," said Marigold. "That old bat was right. I'm not a fit mother."

"Yes you are!" I argued.

I tried to cuddle up close to her when we were back in the flat. I held her tight but I still couldn't get close enough. I pulled her arms round me but after a few seconds they flopped to her sides. I begged her to talk to me but the voice she replied in didn't seem to belong to her. Her eyes were dull and dark, barely green.

"Do you want to go back to bed?" I said. "You look ever so tired."

She went to bed obediently and closed her eyes at once. I leant over her and kissed her on the forehead.

"I said some stupid stuff about you but it was just to make Star come back," I whispered.

Marigold didn't reply but a tear trickled beneath one of her eyelids.

"I think I'll go to bed too," I said.

I huddled up in my strange lonely room. I played games inside my head, pretending I had discovered a secret time machine. If I touched a special stud on my mattress I hurtled forward ten years and grew willowy and beautiful with long thick hair down to my waist.

Not fair like Star. Red like Marigold? No, as I got older my mousey hair would darken and I'd be raven black at twenty, with my own green eyes outlined with sooty lashes. I'd have clear white skin with just one exquisite secret tattoo on my shoulder, a little black witch. I'd have a nose stud too, an emerald to match my eyes, but I'd take it out at work and wear sleeves and tie my long black hair into a chic twirl on top. I'd wear black jeans and a black smock and have my own magical hair salon where I'd invent wonderful exotic styles for very special people. I'd adorn hair with flowers and little crystals and beadwork, I'd dye it fantasy shades of purple and turquoise and sky blue, I'd cut and color and crimp all day while models and rock stars and fashion editors fawned all over me and famous photographers recorded my creations.

I'd be taken out by a different dynamic man every single night of the week and I'd allow them to buy me food and flowers and fine wines, but then I'd go home to my beautiful stylish designer flat, silver and black with a mirror ball revolving in each ceiling so that sparkles of light glimmered in every room. Star and Marigold would be there, desperate to please me. If I wasn't too tired I'd maybe be persuaded to style their hair or paint a nail polish design on their fingertips. They'd be so grateful to me and they'd beg me to promise to stay with them forever and ever. . . .

I fell asleep dreaming this and then kept half waking

in the night, not sure whether I was still dreaming or not. I thought I heard Marigold in the kitchen, but when I stumbled in there myself to get a glass of water there was no sign of her. I drank a lot, the glass clinking against my teeth. My tummy rumbled and I remembered I hadn't had any tea. I wondered if I should try to eat something now but the smell of paint was making me feel sick. It seemed stronger than ever, harsh in my nostrils, making my eyes water.

I needed to go to the bathroom after gulping down all the water. I opened the door and saw a white ghost in the moonlight. A ghost. Really there. Glowing eerily white.

I screamed.

The ghost gasped too.

I knew that sound. I knew that smell.

I pulled the light cord and stared at the white figure before me.

"Marigold?"

I couldn't believe what I saw. She was white all over. Even part of her hair. Her neck, her arms, her bare body, her legs. She'd painted herself white with the gloss paint. There were frantic white splotches all over her body, covering each and every tattoo, although the larger darker ones showed through her new white skin like veins.

I put out my hand to touch her, to see if it was real.

"No. Don't. Not dry yet," said Marigold. "Not dry. Wet. So I can't sit down. I can't lie down. I can't. But that's OK. It will dry and so will I. And then I'll be right. I'll be white. I'll be a good mother and a good girlfriend and Micky will bring Star back and we'll be together forever and ever, a family, my family, and it will be all right, it will, it will, I will it, it has to be better. It couldn't be worse, this is a curse. But it will be better better better, no more tattoos, Star hated them, she hated me, but now they're gone, until the laser, could I use a razor? No, too red, I want white, pure light, that's right. . . ."

She went on and on muttering weird half rhymes to herself. I stood shivering beside her. She had gone really mad now. Crazy. Bonkers. Bats.

FROG

I ran the bath with hot water but she wouldn't get in. I tried scrubbing at her with a washcloth but she started screaming. I hung on her ghostly arm and tried to pull her to bed but she stood rigidly, her white feet tensed on the cold linoleum tiles as if they'd taken root. I was scared to leave her by herself as I had no idea what she'd do next. I eventually emptied the bath, dried it with her towel and then curled up inside it with my head on my own towel. It was like being in an iron cradle and I didn't see how I could ever sleep, with my mad mother palely luminous in the dark. I dozed off when it was starting to get light and then woke with a start, banging my head against the tap. She was still there, swaying slightly, her eyes closed.

"Marigold?"

She opened her eyes. They looked glazed.

"Marigold, please." I struggled out of the bath and took hold of her white shoulders. "Are you asleep?"

Her eyes blinked but she didn't focus on me.

"Let's get it all off you now," I said.

It looked much worse in the daylight. Even her eyelashes were painted like snowy mascara and there were swirls of it inside the delicate skin of her ear.

"Oh, Marigold, what have you *done*? It's gone all over. What if it makes you go blind or deaf? It's dangerous. Oh please, let's get it off you quick."

I was shaking, wondering how I could have been so stupid just to leave her like that half the night. It had been almost like a dream but now it was horribly real. I was so scared I had to use the loo right in front of her because my whole insides had turned to water. She didn't seem to notice.

As soon as I could I ran the bath again. She was still so stiff I couldn't make her step inside. I scrubbed at her where she stood but it was useless. I only got rid of a few flakes of paint.

I scrabbled desperately in the cupboard under the sink and found an old bottle of turpentine. I poured some on a cloth and started scrubbing at her foot. She flinched at each stroke. The white still wouldn't come off properly but where some of it was streaking her own skin was burning scarlet. I didn't know if it was because of the turpentine. I could be hurting her even more.

"I don't know what to do," I said. "Tell me what to do, Marigold. Please, please."

Her lips moved as if she were whispering but no sound came out.

"Does it hurt? Look, I'll wash the turpentine off. I'm so scared it's burning you." I washed her foot over and over again, until she was standing in a large puddle. The paint was still an ugly white smear, the skin very red underneath apart from a dark patch by her toe. I started, terrified it was something awful like gangrene but then I saw a tiny webbed hand and I remembered the little green frog tattooed between her big toe and her first toe.

She quivered when I touched it. Her lips moved again.

"What? I can't hear you. Can you try louder?"

I straightened up and stood on tiptoe, trying to get up to her level. I stared at her mouth but it didn't make any recognizable shapes of words. I looked at her eyes. I saw how frightened she was too.

"I'm going to get help," I said. "You come and lie down in bed."

She still wouldn't move so I wrapped her up in a towel. Then I kissed her poor crazy white face and ran out of the room. Out of the flat, down the stairs. Not

Mrs. Luft. No. Out the front door, down the road, to the corner and the shops. Any of the shopkeepers? No. All the way to school—and Oliver? Maybe Mr. Harrison? No.

"What am I going to do? Oh Star, why aren't you here, you mean hateful pig? I need you so. I don't know what to *do.*"

I knew what to do. I knew it was the only thing to do. But I felt I was betraying Marigold as I stood in the phone box and dialed the three numbers.

"Emergency?"

"Yes. Yes, it is an emergency," I said. "I think I need an ambulance."

I was connected to someone else who started asking me questions.

"This person's covered in paint," I said. "It won't come off. No, it's not my little brother or sister. It's my mum. No, she can't come in herself. She . . . she can't move. She's sort of stuck. And she won't speak to me anymore. I'm scared she maybe can't hear because the paint's in her ears and everywhere. We live at Flat B, 35 Beacon Road. Please. Will you come?"

I put the phone down and then raced back home. I pounded up the stairs and through the door. Marigold was in the bathroom, standing like a marble statue. I threw myself at her, nearly toppling us both onto the floor.

"Oh, Marigold. Quick, we have to get you dressed.

They're coming. I'm sorry, I know you'll be so mad at me, but the paint's all over you and it's got to be cleaned off. Look at your poor eyes, your poor ears. But once they've done that it'll be all over and you can come back and I'll look after you. We'll be OK, you and me, but you just have to go to get the paint off. Please don't be cross with me. I know you hate hospitals."

As soon as I said the word she started quivering. She didn't say anything, she didn't push me away, she didn't try to get dressed. She just shook all over.

"I'm sorry, I'm so sorry," I sobbed. I ran to get clothes for her but it was going to be too much of a struggle to get her arms and legs in and out of things so I ended up maneuvering her trembly arms into her dressing gown and tying it tight round her painted body. I knew she wouldn't be able to manage her own high heels so I got an old pair of sneakers of Star's. They were a size too small but I managed to wedge Marigold's smeared white feet into them.

Then, before I had time to make any kind of proper plan, there was a knock at the front door.

"I'll have to go to let them in. We don't want Mrs. Luft gawping," I said. "Oh, Marigold. Don't shake. It will all be all right, I swear it will. They'll just get the paint off and then you can come back home."

Marigold looked into my eyes. I felt as if I'd stabbed her through the heart.

"I *had* to," I said, and then I ran to open the door. There were two ambulance people, a man and a woman.

"She's upstairs," I whispered, but as they came into the hallway Mrs. Luft opened her door and peered out, curlers clamped to her head like little metal caterpillars. Her mouth opened when she saw the uniform.

"Oh my lord, what's that crazy woman done now?" she asked the air in front of her.

The ambulance people took no notice. As we went up our flight of stairs the woman patted me on the shoulder.

"Don't worry, poppet," she said cheerily.

She didn't start when she saw my poor mad mother covered in paint.

"Right, dear. We'll soon get you cleaned up. You come with us. Would you like to walk? We can carry you in our chair if you'd sooner?"

Marigold's eyes swiveled but she said nothing. The woman put her hand gently on her elbow. She tried to urge Marigold forward. Nothing happened.

"Come on, now. We don't want to have to haul you about, my love, especially not in front of your little girl." The ambulance lady looked at me. "What about you, chum? Is there anyone to look after you?"

I thought quickly. If I said no then she'd get in touch with the social services and I'd be put in a home.

"Oh yes," I said. "Yes, there's someone to look after me."

I didn't sound terribly convincing. The ambulance people exchanged glances.

"My dad," I said.

They looked relieved.

"Where's Dad now?" the woman persisted.

"Oh, he's at work. On his shift. He'll be home any minute," I said, the lying getting easier.

I looked at Marigold. I wasn't sure she was taking in what I was saying. She was still shaking badly. Her face twitched when I reached up to kiss her.

"I love you," I whispered.

I wanted her to say it back. I wanted her to put her painted arms round me and hug me tight. I wanted her to step out of her sickness and tell them that I'd never so much as set eyes on my father. I wanted her to tell them that she couldn't leave me all on my own.

Her green eyes looked at me but she didn't say a word.

The ambulance people gave up trying to coax her and strapped her into the chair. Her dressing gown fell apart so that her white breasts shone in full view.

"Let's get you decent, dear," said the ambulance lady, tucking the dressing gown over her and up round her chin. It was as if Marigold had shrunk into babyhood.

They carried her out of the room, down the stairs, along the hall. I followed them to the front door. Mrs. Luft was still lurking. When she saw the state of Marigold she hissed with excitement.

"Can the little girl stay with you till Dad gets back?" said the ambulance woman.

Mrs. Luft made a little chew-swallow-murmur, as if she were snacking on her own false teeth.

The ambulance people took this for a yes. They lifted Marigold out of the doorway. When she saw the white ambulance her face screwed up. Tears ran down her cheeks. Her eyes stared at me as they put her in the back.

"I'm sorry," I said.

It was such a silly small word for what I felt.

They shut her inside. The ambulance man gave me the thumbs-up sign.

"Don't worry, kid. It'll be all right. We'll soon get Mum sorted out," he said.

He got into the ambulance and drove off.

"You won't get that one sorted out, not in a month of Sundays," Mrs. Luft snorted.

"You shut up, you nasty mean old moo!"

"*Well!*" She drew herself up, her nostrils pinched white as if I were a bad smell. "There's gratitude! When I've agreed to keep my eye on you until someone comes to look after you."

"I don't need looking after. I can look after myself," I said fiercely.

"Oh yes, little Miss Spitfire. Very funny. How old are you? Ten? Don't be so silly. We'd better phone the welfare people."

"No! No, don't." I swallowed. *"Please* don't. Look, my mum will be back by the time I get home from school, and anyway, there's my dad. Yeah, my dad."

"I don't know. There's no sign of this dad of yours all the time you've been living here. Lots of *uncles*, of course, flitting in and out, but the less said about that the better. I suppose your dad is the one that fancies himself with the pretty-boy hair and silly clothes. *I* saw you all. Is he the one?"

I nodded, wishing Micky really were my dad. Then he'd be looking after me and telling me what to do about Marigold. I had to get away from Mrs. Luft before I started crying again.

"I'm going to school," I said quickly. "I've got to go, I'm ever so late. I'll get into trouble."

I did get into trouble too. Miss Hill was halfway through the first lesson when I got there.

"For goodness' sake, Dolphin! Why are you so late?"

I stood still, wondering what I could possibly say.

"This really isn't good enough. Did you oversleep?"

This seemed the best option so I nodded.

"Then you must go to bed earlier. What time did you go to bed last night?'

I thought about it. I couldn't remember exactly. Half the night I wasn't even *in* bed, I was curled up in the bath trying to keep a watch over Marigold.

I could see a pale ghost of her even now in the classroom. I could feel my eyes watering. I sniffed and wiped my nose with the back of my hand.

"Really! Don't you have a tissue? Look at the state of you. You look as if you've tumbled straight out of bed. You haven't even brushed your hair or washed your face, have you?"

Yvonne and Kayleigh started sniggering as she got stuck into me. I held my face tight to stop myself crying. I fingered my witchy black velvet, trying to summon up evil powers, but I couldn't make anything work. Miss Hill went on and on, telling me it just wasn't good enough, I was a dirty lazy girl without any sense of pride and if I didn't wipe that insolent smirk off my face she'd send me straight to the head teacher.

I swiveled my head to try to change my expression. I saw a blurry view of the class, lots of them grinning and giggling, but then I saw a flash of glass. I blinked and saw Oliver clearly, his face white and tense, his eyes big behind his specs. He looked so sorry for me that I couldn't bear it. I suddenly started howling.

"Really, Dolphin! There's no need for tears," said Miss Hill. She was still scornful, but she sounded a bit scared too, as if she realized she'd gone too far. "Stop that silly crying now."

I couldn't stop. I snorted and sobbed, my nose running.

"Here." I felt a hankie being pressed into my hand. I opened my teary eyes. It was Oliver.

"Sit down, Oliver. And you, Dolphin. Shall we get on with our work, everybody?"

I squeezed Oliver's hand and then went to sit down, mopping my face.

Kayleigh and Yvonne whispered all sorts of stuff about me being a baby and dirty and snotty.

"Snottle Bottle Nose," Kayleigh said, and they both burst out laughing.

"That's enough, Yvonne and Kayleigh. Settle down at once," said Miss Hill.

I didn't even turn round to stick my tongue out at them to show I was glad they'd got into trouble. I couldn't be bothered with any of this school stuff anymore. I just kept thinking of Marigold and wondering what they were doing to her. Why hadn't I gone with her to the hospital?

At morning break I shot off quickly, not wanting to be with anyone, not even Oliver. But he caught up with me and cornered me.

"I didn't think anyone could make you cry," he said.

"Yes, well, they can't. Especially not hateful Bumface Hill. I was crying about something else, OK?" I said, clenching my fists.

"What else?" said Oliver. "Don't get mad at me, Dolphin. I'm your friend."

"I know. I'm sorry. It's just . . . oh, Owly, I don't know what to do."

"Oliver!"

"Sorry. I wasn't thinking. It's my mum."

"I thought it was."

"I phoned the ambulance to come and get her. I *had* to, because of all the paint, in her ears and eyes and everywhere, but now she'll never forgive me."

"What?" said Oliver, blinking behind his glasses.

I explained.

"I feel so terrible. She hates hospitals."

"But you had to. You did the right thing, Dolphin, honestly."

"Do you think I should bunk off school and go to the hospital now, to be with her?"

"Maybe they wouldn't let you see her. If they're scrubbing off all the paint. Wait a bit. Let me think. Here, have you still got my hankie? I think you need to use it again."

"Oh, Oliver." I hung on to him because there was no one else.

"Yuck! Look! Bottle Nose and Owly are snogging again!" Yvonne and Kayleigh and a whole little gang of girls were fast approaching.

"You shut up, you stupid Piddle Pants," I yelled. "If

you say one more thing I'll smash your stupid teeth in—and then no one will ever want to snog *you*."

I rounded on them so determinedly that they scattered.

"You are *fierce*, Dolphin," said Oliver. "I'm glad you're on *my* side."

"I'm glad you're on mine," I said. "You'll help me sort out what to do?"

"Well . . . I'll try."

"You've got the mega-whizzo brainpower, right?"

"Right," said Oliver. "OK. Leave it to me."

The rest of the morning went so s-l-o-w-l-y it seemed as if it were already the summer holidays when the bell rang for lunchtime. I looked at Oliver expectantly.

"We'll phone the hospital," he said.

It didn't seem much of a solution to all the black worries buzzing in my head, but it seemed like a good starting point. I didn't have any money but Oliver had a good supply of ten and twenty pences. I needed most of them too, because the hospital switchboard kept me waiting ages while they looked up Marigold's name and tried to track her down. They put me through to Casualty and they checked and eventually said she wasn't there anymore.

"So she's home already!" I said. I felt the tight band round me loosen so that my heart gave a happy thump.

"No . . ."

My heart clamped.

"Where is she then?"

"She's been admitted to Tennyson."

"Tennyson?"

"I'll put you through."

So I waited again, wondering what had gone wrong now. Maybe Tennyson was a special ear, nose and throat ward and they were checking in case the paint had done any damage. Or maybe Tennyson was the eye ward and they were using special eye baths to get the paint off her lashes?

Maybe.

Maybe I knew perfectly well what sort of ward it was.

"Tennyson Psychiatric Ward. How can I help you?"

I pressed the phone hard against my ear. I didn't want Oliver to know.

"I think—there's this lady, she's called Marigold, Marigold Westward. She—she might be having treatment?"

"Ah! Yes. Yes, we admitted a Ms. Westward to the ward this morning."

"And—and will she be better soon?"

"I think it might take a while. Who's speaking, please? Are you Ms. Westward's little girl?"

"No. No, I'm grown up, I just sound young," I said, trying to deepen my voice.

I turned my back on Oliver because he was putting me off.

"Well, we need to speak to an adult family member about Ms. Westward," the voice said gently.

"I'm adult. And family. I'm—I'm her sister. Is she going to be able to come home tonight? I can look after her and give her any medicine she needs. But she really hates it in hospital, you see. It's actually bad for her to be in hospital. So if you've got all the paint off, can't she come home? Now?"

"I'm afraid not, dear. Ms. Westward is really quite seriously ill at the moment."

"What has she got? Is it poisoning from the paint?"

"No, no. I really don't think I should discuss this on the phone. Perhaps you could come and have a chat with us?"

"I . . . Please! Can't you just tell me when she'll be home? Tomorrow? The day after? *When?*"

"It's impossible to say. We can't make any predictions. But I shouldn't imagine it will be too long. A matter of weeks."

"*Weeks!*"

"I think you *are* very young, dear. Where are you ringing from? Do you have an adult with you? Listen, dear—"

I didn't dare listen anymore. I slammed the phone down. I shut my eyes to try to blot everything out. It was very silent in the corridor because everyone else was at lunch. I could just hear Oliver breathing heavily beside me.

"Weeks?" he whispered.

"Yes." I opened my eyes. It was no use trying to kid him. "She's in the nutty ward. I expect she's locked up. Oh, Owly, what am I going to do?"

He didn't blink at the unintentional "Owly."

"We'll think of something," he said, trying to sound reassuring.

"I can't stay at home by myself for weeks. Mrs. Luft will phone the welfare. And I haven't got any money. I won't be able to go down the post office for the check because it's Marigold who has to collect it, kids aren't allowed, I know, because Star tried once." I started shaking when I said Star's name.

"Can't you go and live with Star and her dad?" said Oliver. "You said she asked you to come too."

"But they don't really want me. And anyway, I don't know where they *are*. She's meant to be sending me a new phone. I could ask her then. She might come back if she believes me. Oh, I *wish* she was here."

"I'm here," said Oliver, patting my arm nervously, as if he were trying to make friends with a snappy little dog.

I looked at him.

"Oliver? Could I . . . could I come and live with you and your mum?"

Oliver's eyes widened.

"Not for good. Just for a few days. Until I can get in touch with Star. Oh please, Oliver, say yes."

"I—I don't . . ."

"I've had you to tea at my house and you can stay over anytime you want. So can't I come to your house? Maybe just for tonight?"

"I wish you could, Dolphin," said Oliver. "But it's my mum. She doesn't want anyone to come round. She just wants it to be her and me. I asked her if I could have you for tea and she just said not at the moment, she wasn't up to it. She's gone a bit funny since my dad left."

"Look, *my* mum's seriously bananas. I'm used to mums being odd. I won't laugh or anything. I'll be ever so good. I'll take my own sleeping bag so I won't even need a bed. Please, Oliver."

"Well, I'll phone and ask. But I don't think she'll say yes."

Oliver phoned. I could hear his mum's startled tone.

"Oliver, darling? Oh my goodness, what's the matter? Why are you phoning? What's happened? Have you hurt yourself?" She asked dozens of questions without letting him answer. He had to blurt it out while she was saying stuff herself so she didn't even hear first time round. Then he had to repeat it.

"Mum. Please. Can my friend Dolphin—you know, I went to tea at her place—well, can she come to tea tonight, please?"

"And to stay over?" I mouthed.

But Oliver's mum wouldn't even consider tea. She spoke in such a loud, whiny voice I could hear her clearly.

"It's out of the question, darling, you know it is, especially today. I've got another migraine. I'll have to make a doctor's appointment. I just can't go on like this."

"But Mum, Dolphin needs to stay somewhere tonight. Please can't she come?"

"Oliver, what on earth's got into you? I've told you what I think about this weird little girl and her bizarre family. Why you had to get mixed up with her I can't imagine."

Oliver wriggled, his eyes swerving past me. He tried again, several times, but it was obvious it was pointless. There was a brief silence after he put the phone down.

"I'm afraid Mum says you can't come," he said eventually in a tiny voice.

"I know. I heard. It's all right."

"It's not all right," said Oliver. "Oh, Dolphin. Look. Maybe we should tell a teacher?"

"What?" I said. "Puh-Lease. Tell Miss Hill!"

"No. Not her. What about Mr. Harrison. He's nice. He'd help."

"He's nice, yes. But how could he help? He's not going to say 'OK, Dolphin, come and kip down at my house for a few weeks until your mum's better.'"

"No, but maybe he'd know what to do."

"Yeah, I know what he'd do. Call social services. And I'd be shoved into a home."

"Well . . . they'd look after you OK, wouldn't they? And it might even be fun. You could be fostered for a bit."

"You've been watching too much television. Look, my mum was in and out of homes and foster places all her life. She said it was the absolute pits. Some of the things she's told Star and me . . . Well, you'd never believe it, Oliver."

"But if it was just for a week or two?"

"But it wouldn't be, would it? If they've got my mum locked up in the nutty ward they're going to say she's an unfit mother. The social services will do this investigation, see, and if they find out that Marigold often goes a bit weird and likes to go out for a drink or two or three, and she sometimes has boyfriends, and—and there's all the credit card stuff she pulls too—they'll never let me go back and live with her ever. And I need to be with her, Oliver. She's my *mum*."

Oliver blinked at me. His eyes went all wavery the way they do when he's thinking hard. I could almost hear his brain going tick-tick-tick inside his head. Then he started as if an alarm had suddenly gone off.

"I know. It's obvious. Your dad."

"What?"

"Your dad. Star's with *her* dad. Can't you get in touch with yours?"

"I told you. I haven't *got* a dad."

"You must have had one once."

"Look. My mum had this quick thing. She hardly knew him. He can't count as a dad."

"So she didn't even know him?"

"She knew his name. Which is why she went out with him. He was called Micky too."

"She went out with him just because he was called Micky?" Oliver repeated.

"Yes. So? You know she's weird."

"That's all you know about your dad? His name's Micky?"

"So I can't exactly track him down, can I? Would all the Mickys in the world who might have had a little fling eleven years ago please step forward! I think not."

"Your mum hasn't ever told you anything else about him?"

"No, not really."

"Didn't you ever ask? He is your dad."

"He's not, I keep telling you. Not like Star's dad. Marigold and Micky, that Micky, they were crazy about each other. It was mad passionate love, they were together *ages* . . ." I faltered, suddenly remembering that Micky said it had only been a few weeks. So how long had Marigold spent with my Micky? Half an hour?

"Where did they meet?"

"I don't know. Yes I do. Swimming. I think this Micky's a good swimmer because I'm not. I hate swimming and Marigold once said that was funny because this other Micky was a brilliant swimmer. I think he even taught swimming."

"Did he teach your mum?"

"I don't know."

I tried to remember what Marigold had said. It was ages ago, when I was first taken swimming by the school, the school before this one. I was scared of putting my head under the water and the other kids laughed at me and then one of the boys ducked me. Marigold was very kind when I told her and said she's always been scared of swimming too but she'd learnt as an adult and now she could swim all sorts of funny strokes and maybe one day I'd be a good swimmer too because my Micky had been. . . .

"Maybe he was the guy who taught her," I said.

"So maybe he still teaches swimming. Hey, we could go to the leisure pool and find out!"

"No we couldn't. It wasn't this pool. We didn't live round here. We lived . . ." I tried to work it out.

We'd lived in so many different places. "I can't remember. Anyway, what does it matter?"

"We'll track him down, you'll see. *Think*, Dolphin."

"How can I think my way back before I was born?"

I knew we lived somewhere near London when I was born. South of the river. But I wasn't sure *where*.

Oliver started suggesting names. He was into trainspotting—typical!—and chanted his way through all the suburban stations from Waterloo. Some sounded familiar, some didn't.

"It's hopeless, Owly."

"*Oliver*. No, it isn't. We could try them all. See if there's a Micky working at their swimming pools."

"What? Go to *all* those places?"

"Phone! Directory Inquiries will give us all the numbers."

"And then what?" I said. "Suppose we did find him? What's he going to do then?"

"Well. He's your dad. You said Star's dad was over the moon when he met her. He was desperate to look after her."

"Yes. Because she's Star. Who's going to want to look after me? And anyway, like I said, he didn't even know Marigold properly. He's probably forgotten all about her."

"You couldn't possibly forget your mum even if you met her for five minutes," said Oliver.

I supposed that made some kind of sense. I wondered if this idea of his made sense too. Deep deep down I'd always had this dream that one day I'd meet my dad, my Micky, and he'd be almost as good as the real first Micky and he'd love me because I was his little girl, his Dolphin. . . .

It was such a deeply embarrassing dream that I hardly ever dared think it. I could feel my face going red. I knew it was sad and pathetic. Star had always sneered at the idea of either of us meeting our dads. That was why it was so unfair when she met her dad and he was like a prince in a fairy tale and she was his long-lost princess. My dad wouldn't be like that. He'd be a frog who never turned into a prince even after a hundred kisses.

No. *I* was the frog child, the sad ugly one no dad could ever want.

"We wouldn't ever find him. It's a chance in a million. And if we did, he wouldn't want me anyway."

"Let's try," Oliver persisted.

He dialed Directory Inquiries and started asking for swimming pool numbers, lots and lots of them. He didn't have any spare paper so he wrote them all the way up his arm. Then when he had a full sleeve of blotchy blue figures he went to the school secretary and got her to change the secret five-pound note in-case-of-emergency he kept in a little purse in his pocket into ten and twenty pences.

"Right, here goes," said Oliver, squinting at his arm and then dialing the first number.

"What are you going to say?"

"Aren't *you* going to say it?" said Oliver.

"I don't know how to put it. I can't just say, 'Hello, are you Micky? Great, well guess what, I'm your long-lost daughter.'"

"I don't see why not," said Oliver, but he agreed to do the talking.

He did a *lot* of talking. We got through the pile of silver at an alarming rate because there were so many stupid pre-recorded messages about swimming times and you had to hang on for ages before they put you through to the main office.

We were down to the last few coins when Oliver tensed and grabbed my arm with his sweaty hand, but it was a Nicky, not a Micky, and it turned out she was a girl.

"This is crazy. We've just wasted all your emergency money mucking about like this," I said.

"This *is* an emergency," said Oliver. "One more."

He dialed again. He listened to all the recorded messages while the minutes ticked away. I started biting a hangnail, tearing at it with my teeth until a long shred of skin ripped off and I started bleeding.

"Don't, Dolphin!" said Oliver primly.

I licked the blood.

"Yuck, you vampire."

I pulled back my lip to make vampire teeth and pretended to bite his neck. And then the voice started speaking. A man.

I stuck my head close so I could hear too.

"New Barnes Leisure Pool. How can I help you?"

"Oh, hello. Look, this sounds a silly question but can you tell me if there's anyone called Micky working as an instructor at your pool?"

"No Mickys," said the voice.

"See," I mouthed at Oliver.

"None at all?" Oliver persisted.

"Well. I'm Michael. I did get called Micky once. But that was ages ago."

"Oh gosh!" said Oliver. "Look, do you mind my asking how long have you worked at the pool?"

"That's easy. Fifteen years, ever since it opened."

"Oh gosh, oh gosh!" Oliver squeaked. "And do you ever remember meeting a lady, a very pretty lady with red hair and lots of tattoos?"

"You mean . . . Marigold?"

SCREAM

Oliver held the phone out to me. I backed away.

"It's *him*," Oliver whispered.

I knew it was him. I took the phone from Oliver and held it to my ear. I heard his voice properly for myself. It sounded so close it tickled.

I slammed the phone back down. Cutting him off. Cutting me off.

Oliver's mouth hung open.

"No, no! It was him, I know it was. He said the name Marigold."

"I know."

"So he must be your dad."

"Maybe."

"So why didn't you *speak* to him?"

"I don't know. I didn't want to. Oh shut up, Owly."

"Oliver! And don't tell me to shut up. I'm trying to *help*." Oliver's lip trembled.

"I'm sorry."

"I don't understand. We tracked him down."

"Look, I just didn't want to say anything. I didn't think in a million years we'd ever find him. Well, maybe we haven't. My mum isn't the only Marigold in the world."

"Oh come *on*, Dolphin."

"And anyway, so what if he did know her? It doesn't prove he's my dad. Maybe Marigold was just making it up about him. She makes up all sorts of stuff. I wonder what they're *doing* to her—"

"Look, Dolphin. You've got to think about you for a bit. If you don't want to see your dad—"

"I've no idea if he *is* my dad."

"All *right*. But if you don't get in touch with him then what are you going to do? Who's going to look after you?"

"I shall look after myself," I said. "If—if you could maybe lend me a little bit of cash, because I don't think we've got much food in, then I'll be fine. I'll stomp about in heavy shoes so that Mrs. Luft thinks I've got someone with me. I'll be OK for a few days and then maybe Marigold will be able to get out of hospital." I tried to make it sound as simple and ordinary and everyday as I could but my voice was getting higher and higher as I thought of staying in the flat all by myself with Mrs. Luft lurking underneath me and the ghost of Mr. Rowling slithering up above.

I stopped. Oliver was looking at me sadly. I couldn't even kid him.

"Haven't you got a granny or aunty or anyone?"

"No. Well. Maybe I have. But Marigold was taken into care, see, so she didn't see her family after that. *She's* just my family. Her and Star."

"And your dad. I could phone him again, Dolphin."

"No. I can't . . . you can't just blurt out stuff on the phone."

"Then see him."

"See him when?"

"We could go there. On the train."

"We haven't got any money."

"Aha!" Oliver delved inside his shoe and came up with *another* five-pound note, tightly folded and a little smelly. "This is my extra emergency money in case I lose my emergency money."

"You're nuts!"

"No I'm not! Come on. Let's go. Now."

"You mean bunk off school?"

"Yes," said Oliver. "Let's. Come on."

I was so startled that goody-goody wimpy little brainbox Oliver was prepared to do such a momentous thing on my behalf that I found myself nodding.

"Right. OK."

So we walked straight out of school. No one said a word as we walked down the corridor, out the entrance, across the playground and out the gate. It was so simple. I wondered why I'd never done it before. Oliver's walk was a bit wobbly, but he grinned at me through gritted teeth.

"This feels so peculiar," I said. "I can't believe we're really doing this. It's like a dream. Maybe it is."

"Shall I pinch you?" Oliver gave me a delicate pinch on the back of my hand.

"Did you feel it?"

"Barely. You're not a very vicious pincher, Oliver."

"Not like Ronnie Churley. He's horrible at pinching."

"Yeah. And his Chinese burns!"

"He kicked me once in the boys' toilets. Right in the stomach. I cried and he called me a baby."

"He's a baby, though, trotting to school with his mum."

"I go to school with my mum. Oh. I've just thought. She'll be coming to meet me at school at half past three."

"Oh. Well. Look, you go back."

"No, I'm coming with you. I can maybe get back in time. Or—or I'll phone her so she doesn't worry. Well, she *will* worry, but it can't be helped."

"She'll say it's that weird little girl's influence."

"Oh. You heard."

"Yep. Never mind. Everyone thinks I'm weird."

"*I* think you're weird but I like it."

"You're actually pretty weird yourself, Oliver. Hey, we're the wondrous weirdos, right?"

"Yes, OK. Dolphin, what if someone stops us and asks us why we're not in school?"

"Easy. We're going to the dentist's."

"What about at the station?"

"They won't ask. Why should they?"

"Well, because we haven't got a grown-up with us. It does feel funny." Oliver swung his arms to show how odd it felt.

"I'm often out without an adult."

"I'm not. In fact, don't laugh, but this is the very first time."

"Now, that *is* weird. Well, don't worry. I'll look after you."

It was Oliver, however, who worked out the train journey because it wasn't as simple as I'd thought. We had to change at Wimbledon and I'd have jumped on the wrong train if Oliver hadn't hung on to me. He bought us two Mars bars and two packets of crisps and two cans of Coke, which used up every last penny of his emergency money.

I was starting to feel a bit sick when we got to New Barnes.

"I'm not sure Mars bars really go with crisps," I

said. "Especially not with Coke on top." I burped miserably.

"You'll be all right in a minute," said Oliver. He asked a lady the way to the leisure pool. She said it wasn't far and we couldn't miss it. We set off walking in the direction she sent us. We walked for quite a bit, not saying much. It seemed far. It looked as if we had missed it.

I didn't mind.

Oliver asked again and then we doubled back on ourselves and saw a big modern white building at the end of the street.

"That looks like it," said Oliver.

I said nothing.

"You're ever so quiet," said Oliver.

"I feel sick. I told you."

"It's probably because you're scared about meeting your dad."

"No, it's not," I said, irritated. "Stop being such a know-all. You don't know anything."

"Yes I do," said Oliver softly. "Scaredy-cat." But he laced his bony little fingers through mine as he said it.

I glared at him but I gripped his hand hard. I hung on tight as we got nearer and nearer the leisure pool. The smell of the chlorine was so strong as we went through the entrance that I wondered if I really was going to throw up.

"Take a deep breath," Oliver advised.

I stood still and gasped as if I were making a dirty phone call.

The woman at the reception desk eyed us up and down.

"Are you both over ten?"

"Of course we are," said Oliver. "But we don't actually want to go for a swim."

"Well, the café's over there."

"No, we don't want the café either."

"Well, if it's the toilets you're not allowed to use them if you're not using the leisure center premises, but your friend looks a bit dodgy, so if she needs to dash into the ladies' I'll turn a blind eye."

"It's kind of you, but she doesn't need the toilet," said Oliver.

"I do," I said truthfully. I did have to make a dash for it.

When I returned, white and trembling, the lady and Oliver looked shocked.

"You look awful," said Oliver.

"Perhaps you'd better come into the office and sit down," said the lady. "I'll ring your mother."

"You can't," I said, and I started crying.

There was a lot of fussing after that. I was led into the office, Oliver holding my hand again, which was kind of him though it meant I couldn't wipe my nose properly. A thin man with big black glasses and a gray tracksuit shook his head at me.

"Dear oh dear, you look a bit woebegone," he said. "What's up?"

"She's not well at all. Can I leave the kids with you a minute, there's a line at the desk. Thanks, Michael."

I stared at him. Michael. My dad.

I'd never had any clear idea what he looked like. Marigold had always described him as nothing special, which wasn't helpful. Then I'd rearranged my ideas over the last couple of hours and pictured him as a brawny bronze hunk in Lycra shorts.

This Michael was a shock.

"You're Michael!" said Oliver.

He stopped looking at me. He stared at Oliver. His face went white.

"You're the kid who phoned," he said.

Oliver nodded.

"You asked if I remembered Marigold." He said it oddly, as if it were a magic name and saying it out loud would make all his wishes come true.

"What's your name, son?" he whispered.

"Oliver," said Oliver.

Michael bent down and clasped Oliver gently by his narrow shoulders.

"I knew it," said Michael. "I knew it as soon as I heard your voice. And now look at you. A real chip off the old block. Oh, Oliver. I'm your dad, aren't I?" He pulled Oliver closer to hug him.

"No!" said Oliver, wriggling out of his grasp.

"I'm sorry, I'm sorry," said Michael, setting him free at once. "I know I can't rush things. This is probably very difficult for you. But ever since Marigold left I've been haunted by the thought of you."

"No! Not me," Oliver said. "I've got my own dad. I'm just her friend. It's *her*."

He took me by the wrist and yanked me upright. I was still feeling so weak I went dizzy. Oliver and Michael started multiplying and spinning round me.

"Sit down and put your head between your legs," said Michael.

"Put my head *where?*" I mumbled.

"To stop you fainting." He took hold of me by the elbows and sat me back down. He gently pressed my head down until my knees nudged my ears.

"There!" he said, as the black whirling slowed down. "OK. You can try putting your head up now."

"Up and down, up and down. I feel like a yo-yo," I said shakily.

"Now," said Michael, sitting on the arm of my chair. "Are you telling me *you're* Marigold's baby?"

"I'm not a baby. I'm nearly eleven." Then I realized what he meant. "How did you know she was having a baby?"

"It was why she left. I was so thrilled, but she didn't know if she could cope. Star was only little. Marigold didn't want—" He stopped suddenly.

I stared at him, rubbing my eyes, trying to get him properly in focus.

"You mean, you and Marigold, you lived together for a bit?"

"Eleven months."

I must have looked astonished.

"I loved her so much," said Michael. "I knew she didn't really care about me. She wanted that Micky. But he didn't want her."

"She's the same now," I said.

"Does she know you're here?" He looked painfully eager. "She's not waiting outside, is she?"

"No. She's—she's in hospital."

"What's wrong with her?"

"She's not very well. Sort of . . . mentally."

"Ah."

"And Star's with Micky now."

"Is she? How did that come about? He left long before she was born."

"Well, he came back. And he's taken Star."

"So Star's got her dad. And—and you came looking for *your* dad. Me."

I felt myself going bright red. Michael had gone through an overly emotional scene with Oliver. It would seem so daft if he repeated it with me.

The weird thing was that Michael and Oliver really did look as if they were related. Michael and I didn't look at all alike. He was dark, I was mousey. He had vague brown eyes, mine were sharp green. He had pink cheeks and I was always white unless I was blushing.

"Maybe you're not my dad," I said. "We don't look like each other."

"You look like Marigold."

I stared at him. My dad was pretty stupid.

"Marigold's beautiful," I said. "I'm ugly."

"No you're not. You're very like her. Your hair, your skin, your eyes."

"Marigold's got red hair," said Oliver.

"It was pale brown when she was with me," said Michael. He smiled at me, his eyes big and blinking behind his black glasses.

"Do you swim wearing your glasses?" I asked.

"I have prescription goggles," he said. "Though I look a bit like a frog in them."

I thought.

"Marigold has a frog tattoo."

"Between her toes. I know. I held her hand when she had it done."

"I have to hold her hand too."

"Has she got a lot more now?"

"She's practically covered up!" said Oliver. "She looks amazing. Like a comic. I'd give anything to have a mum who looks like that. Oh, *my* mum! Do you think I could possibly make a quick phone call?"

"Of course."

While Oliver was dialing and then spinning his

mum some long involved story Michael and I looked at each other. Then we looked away. Then we looked at each other again.

"I don't know your name!" he said suddenly.

"It's Dolphin."

"Dolphin," he said slowly, trying it out.

"It's a stupid name."

"No it's not."

"The kids call me Bottle Nose at school."

"Well, they're stupid. Dolphins are beautiful animals anyway."

"Fish."

"No, they're mammals. Highly intelligent. And amazing in the water. Do you like swimming, Dolphin?"

"I can't."

"You can't *swim*?" He'd taken on board a bogus son and a probable daughter without turning a hair but now he sounded genuinely astonished. "I don't believe it. Didn't Marigold teach you? I taught *her*."

"We don't ever go swimming. I did with the school, but it was mostly just messing about."

"I'll teach you," said Michael.

I swallowed. The swirling feeling was starting up again.

"So can I come and stay with you? Just for a bit? Till Marigold gets better?"

Michael swallowed too. His Adam's apple bobbed about in his throat.

"Well, yes. Of course. But there's all sorts of things that will have to be sorted out first."

It was simple when it came to Micky and Star. It was very very very complicated with Michael and me.

"We've got to do things properly, Dolphin."

"Properly" meant he had to take us back to school, go to the hospital, see a social worker there, see another special children's social worker, see the entire social services to sort out what was going to be done.

"No!" I wailed. "No, please don't. *Not* the social."

"We've got to do things the right way. I can't just take you out of the blue. We're strangers, even if we are father and daughter." He said the words stiltedly, going a bit pink.

"Micky just took Star."

"Yes. That figures. But Micky seems to have a habit of rushing in—and then rushing off, leaving all kinds of havoc behind him. I want to do this my way."

"But it's not *my* way. I'm not seeing any social workers. They'll just take me into care and they *don't* care. They smack you and they tell you off and if you wet the bed they put the sheet over your head."

"Do you wet the bed, Dolphin?" Oliver asked with interest.

"No! But that's what it's like in homes. Marigold said. And she should know, she's been in heaps."

"But that was a while ago. Things have changed. And anyway, you're not *going* to end up in a home. You can stay with me if the social workers think it's suitable and I'll have to discuss it with my family too, of course."

The word "family" hit me like a pile of bricks.

"Family?"

"Yes. I've got a wife, Meg, and two daughters, Grace and Alice."

The words struck me on the head. Wife, bang. Daughters, bang bang.

That was why he was so thrilled when he thought Oliver was his son. He didn't need another daughter.

"It's OK," I said. "It was a mad idea coming here. Not *my* idea. We don't need you to take us back. We've got return tickets, haven't we, Oliver?"

"Well, yes," said Oliver. "And actually I'd sooner we didn't go back to *school* because I've just told my mum this long story about a school trip to a leisure center—it wasn't *exactly* a lie—and how the bus would drop me off right at the end of our street but they couldn't say the exact time and she only half seemed to believe me and she gets very upset. You know what she's like, Dolphin."

Oliver rambled on about his mum. I didn't take much of it in. Michael wasn't listening either. He was fumbling through a little plastic wallet.

"Here," he said, and he showed me this photo of him in some silly cycling stuff and a blond wife in pink shorts and two fair girls with big eyes and pointy chins in T-shirts and flowery leggings.

"Here they are. Grace is seven and Alice is five."

I didn't say anything.

"They're your half sisters."

I looked at these strange girls. They didn't really look anything to do with me.

"This was taken when we were on this crazy camping holiday last year. We all took our bikes and went all over the place, even Alice."

"I can't ride a bike," I said.

"I could teach you. Hey, you could maybe come camping with us sometime."

"Meg won't like that idea."

Michael looked me straight in the eyes.

"It might be a bit difficult at first. Meg knows all about Marigold but she's always felt . . . worried about her."

I suddenly saw Marigold, lots of Marigolds. Marigold painted white like a ghost, Marigold all dressed up and going out on the town, Marigold wincing in pain as she got herself tattooed, Marigold yelling at me, Marigold hiding under the sheets, Marigold making the cake house in the field, all my Marigolds.

"I want Marigold," I said.

"We'll go and see her," said Michael. "I'll tell them that I have to get off work now. I'll take you both back. Don't worry, son, I'll drop you off at your home."

I still thought he said the word "son" wistfully, as if

he wanted to pop a "my" in front. He'd have sooner had Oliver than me. I didn't ever come first with anyone. I was always second best.

When Michael went off to tell some colleagues he was leaving work early Oliver gave me a quick hug.

"He's nice, Dolphin, he really is. He'll look after you. It's going to be all right. It was a good idea of mine to find him, wasn't it?"

"OK, OK, it was a great idea," I said, and I hugged him back.

He was quite a bit smaller than me so his fluffy hair got up my nose.

"Your hair's tickling, Oliver!"

Oliver dodged away, smoothing his hair self-consciously. His bangs were so long now, they hung over his glasses.

"Why don't you get them cut?"

"I know. I keep telling my mum, but she can never get it organized."

"Why doesn't she cut it?"

"Her hands are so shaky I'd end up with the bangs all zigzag and my ears snipped off."

"I'll cut it for you sometime," I offered. "I'm good at cutting hair, honest."

I picked up a lock of his hair and made professional scissor movements with my fingers.

"Playing hairdressers?" said Michael, coming back into the office. "Meg's a hairstylist, Dolphin."

"Is she?" I said it flatly, as if I weren't the slightest bit interested.

There was no point hoping she'd take me along to her salon and show me stuff. Even Michael had agreed there would be problems with Meg. I was sure she'd hate me.

It was quite a long drive back. Oliver was in the front with Michael. They chatted away endlessly. They were both computer freaks and so they went on about the Internet and all these different games and systems. I got so bored I huddled up in the back and pretended to be asleep.

"Dolphin's nodded off," said Oliver after a while.

"Maybe," said Michael.

"It's so great she's found you. It was all *my* idea."

"I know it was, Oliver. A very good idea."

"You are pleased, aren't you?"

"I'm very pleased. Of course I am. Though it's all a bit hard to take in. I mean, I hadn't properly thought about Marigold in a long while. After she left I did nothing but search for her, but then after a year or so I knew I had to make a new life for myself or I'd go crazy. I met Meg and we got together and had the girls. And now it turns out I've got three girls."

"Dolphin's a very special girl," said Oliver. "You'll like her lots and lots. I do."

I felt tears pricking inside my eyelids. Maybe I came first with Oliver.

I had to open my eyes when we got back to our town and Oliver started directing Michael to the road where he lived. I didn't want him to go. I felt worried about it being just Michael and me.

"Bye-bye then," said Oliver, as he got out of the car. "It was very nice to meet you, Michael. Maybe I could have some swimming lessons too?"

"You bet, son."

"You're sure you'll be all right now, Dolphin?"

"Sure," I said, though I'd never felt less sure about anything.

"Oh well. I'd better get going. I'm not sure my mum's going to believe a word of my story. So. I'll see you at school, Dolphin?"

"Yep."

"Right."

He still dithered, peering at me through the window. Then he waved wildly, though the car wasn't moving. I waggled my fingers back at him, and Michael drove off.

"We'll go to the hospital first. Any idea where it is?" said Michael.

I was glad I had to direct him. It meant we didn't have to try to make conversation. I was also getting worried about the trip to the hospital.

"What's it like?" I said. "You know, the loony ward."

"I don't know, but I don't think we should call it that."

"Will everyone be in those white strappy things like corsets?"

"Straitjackets? No, I'm sure they won't be. It'll probably be like an ordinary hospital ward."

"Only everyone will be mumbling and staring and doing stupid stuff."

"I shouldn't think so. But if you're really worried you don't have to come in. You can stay in the car. Maybe children aren't allowed on the ward in any case."

"No, I'd better come. I want to see Marigold," I said, though I was sure she wasn't going to want to see me.

It took us ages to find the right ward and then when we got there at last, a nurse bustling past frowned at me.

"I'm not sure about the little girl," she said. "We tend to stick to over-fourteens, unless there's a very special reason."

"Oh, there *is* a special reason this time. Dolphin's mother was taken into hospital this morning and she's been very worried about her. She badly needs to see her," said Michael.

"Ah. We're talking about Marigold, right? The lady with . . ." She gestured to her arms and legs as if inking instant tattoos in the air. Then she suddenly smiled at Michael. "Hey, you're not the Micky she keeps going on about?"

"I wish I was," said Michael.

I stared at him. Maybe it had been hard for him being second best too.

"So who are you?" said the nurse.

"He's my dad," I said.

The nurse told us Marigold was in a bed at the end of the ward.

"She's still feeling a bit groggy because they had to give her quite a going-over to get all the paint off. And she's still very high too."

"High?" said Michael.

"She means drunk," I said.

"No, no. High, manic, deluded, agitated. But don't worry. She'll respond to the lithium we're giving her."

"She won't want to take it," I said.

"We know that all right! There's been a little battle," said the nurse. "But if she keeps on her lithium she'll soon get used to the side effects and it'll be such a help. Many people with bipolar disorder lead perfectly normal lives."

"My mum's never been normal in her life," I said, and I set off to look for her.

Most of the beds were empty. I could see a big room off to the side where people were gathered together in a circle, someone talking, someone else crying. She wasn't there. She didn't seem to be in the ward. Then I thought about the drawn curtains at the end. I put my eye to the crack. I saw a flash of color.

"Marigold!" I stepped inside.

She was lying on the bed in a strange white nightie. She was no longer white herself. Her skin still had a raw pink scrubbed look in between her tattoos. One of her arms was nearly covered now, a full sleeve. She was inking in all the gaps with a ballpoint pen. It was the same tattoo over and over again, like a wallpaper design. A weird woman cowering, her mouth open wide in an awful scream.

"Marigold?" I whispered.

She didn't react.

"Marigold!" I said, louder.

She went on drawing. She finished one screamer and immediately started on another.

I wondered if the paint had done serious damage to her hearing.

"Look who's here," I said.

She looked, her head swiveling round. It was obvious who she wanted it to be. When she saw the man behind me wasn't Micky she turned back straightaway and went on inking. She could hear all right. She just didn't want to hear me. Or Michael.

"Hello, Marigold. It's me, Michael. Well, you called me Micky. I'm . . . Dolphin's father?" He said it with a question in his voice.

Marigold wasn't prepared to give him an answer. She went on inking.

"You shouldn't do that. Your skin's sore from scrubbing the paint off. You'll hurt yourself," I said.

Marigold stabbed at her skin with the pen point. It looked as if that was the whole idea. Maybe she wanted to hurt me too. I was the one who put her in the place she hated most.

"I'm sorry," I whispered. "You had to go into hospital. I didn't know what else to do. Please don't be so cross with me."

I felt a hand pressing my shoulder.

"It's not your fault, Dolphin," said Michael. "It's not Marigold's either. She's very sick at the moment. But she'll get better. Do you hear that, Marigold? You'll get better and you'll be able to look after your girls, but until then I'll keep an eye on Dolphin, so you needn't worry about her."

Marigold didn't look as if she were doing any worrying about me whatsoever. Michael gave my shoulder a final squeeze and then bent toward the figure on the bed.

"I wish you hadn't run away from me," he said. "Especially when you know yourself how much it hurts. But I'm so glad you kept Dolphin. I know you've got your life and I've got mine but we are both her parents and I hope one day we can be friends."

Marigold made an odd little sound. It could have been a snort or a sob.

246

"I'll bring Dolphin to see you soon," he said. "She's missing you very much. Maybe you'll try to get better quickly for her?"

It didn't look to me as if Marigold could ever get better. I cried when we came out of the ward.

"You'll think I blub all the time and yet I hardly ever cry," I sniffed.

"I know," said Michael. "You've had a really tough day. Anyone would cry."

His hands flapped toward me. I wanted a hug but he ended up giving my shoulders another fierce squeeze. I felt as if I were being pegged on a clothes-line.

"Now. What are we going to do with you?" he said.

DIAMONDS

Guess what. I ended up in a foster home.

"It's just a temporary thing, until we get everything sorted out," said Lizzie, the social worker.

"I'll come and see you as often as I can," said Michael. "Don't look so frightened. And when I've talked things over with Meg and the girls you can come and visit, stay overnight, maybe stay awhile longer if that's what you'd like."

"I want to stay now," I mumbled.

"Dolphin, it's too soon. We're still total strangers. And both Meg and I are out all day. It's too far for you to travel backward and forward to your school and the hospital."

"Michael's right, Dolphin. This is the only way to do things. I know your sister went off with her dad but we badly need to get in touch with her too so we can keep an eye on things."

"You won't be able to track her down," I said.

There was a parcel from Star waiting at home for me. We went there so I could get my nightie and toothbrush and stuff.

I opened up the big cardboard box and saw the mobile phone. There was a note inside to say it had been charged and that I was to switch it on straightaway. I didn't see the point. She probably wouldn't believe me if I told her the absolute truth now. And I wanted her to feel bad and worry about why she couldn't ring me. It was all right for her, living her fairy-tale life with Micky. I was the one about to be locked up in a witch's dungeon and fed bread and water.

"What about a special toy?" said Lizzie. "Oh, how about this lovely dolphin!"

"I hate it," I said, throwing it hard against the wall. I snatched up my silk scarf instead, hoping they'd think it was just a hankie.

"What about your jeans and sneakers? Leggings and T-shirts? Clean socks? A woolly cardi?" said Michael, looking round my bedroom sadly.

I pictured his girls, Grace and Alice, in their jeans from Gap and Nike sneakers, their flowery leggings and cute emblem T-shirts, their clean white socks, their cuddly cardigans knitted by their mum . . .

"I don't wear those sort of clothes. This is what I

wear," I said, crossing my arms and hugging my black witch dress.

"Right. Yes. Well, it's very . . . attractive," Michael said, trying hard. He obviously thought my dress hideous.

Maybe I did too. It didn't seem to have any witchly power left whatsoever.

"OK then. We'd better make a move," said Lizzie. "We can pop back in a couple of days if there's anything else you need."

She let me lock the flat up and keep the key.

"It's your home, Dolphin, not mine," said Lizzie.

"I'm sure you'll be able to come back really soon," said Michael. "Well. I'll come and see you tomorrow, OK? Lizzie's given me the address. Dolphin? You're not really scared about the foster home, are you?"

I didn't bother replying. We both knew just how scared I was.

"I'll say goodbye then," said Michael, dithering. He looked at Lizzie as if he were asking her permission to clear off.

"Right. Don't worry. Off you go," she said.

Michael stayed a further five minutes, fussing about this and that, checking phone numbers and addresses, asking me three more times if I was all right when I was all wrong wrong wrong.

Then he said one final goodbye, poking his head

through Lizzie's car window. He aimed clumsily at my cheek, giving it a dry kiss. I didn't make any attempt to kiss him back. After all, he was abandoning me. He didn't want me even though he was my dad.

He didn't feel like my dad one little bit.

"He seems such a nice man, your dad," said Lizzie as we drove off.

I sniffed. "He's OK, I suppose." I bit my hangnail. "I bet that's the last I see of him."

"No, you're wrong there, Dolphin. Are you *really* called Dolphin or is it a nickname? No, your dad is serious about all this. That's why he wants to do it all by the book. He's obviously very keen to welcome you into his life but this has all happened so quickly. He needs to have time to adjust, and a chance to prepare his family."

"What about my adjusting time?' I said. "It's happened quickly to me too."

"Yes, I know. You're holding up very well."

I didn't feel as if I were holding up at all. I cowered down in my seat and thought about the Foster Mother. I pictured her tall and thin with a frowny forehead and a tight mouth. She had hard hands for smacking and she smelt of disinfectant.

I thought about going to bed. I hadn't been 100 percent truthful with Oliver. I wondered about fashioning big holes in my plastic carrier bag and wearing it over my knickers in bed, just in case. Although the other kids would see and tease. I pictured the other foster kids. They were like Ronnie Churley and Yvonne and Kayleigh but bigger and tougher and much much meaner. I pictured the foster home itself, big and bare and bleak, with a terrible black basement where persistently naughty children were tied up as a punishment.

"We're nearly there now," Lizzie said brightly, offering me a Rollo packet. "Take two."

The chocolate and toffee glued my teeth together. I started to feel carsick. I stared straight ahead, prickling with sweat.

I pictured the meeting with the Foster Mother.

"This is your foster mother, Dolphin. Shake hands nicely and say hello."

I'd open my mouth and spray her skirt with chocolate vomit and get sluiced down and shoved in the basement in double-quick time.

"Here we are," said Lizzie. "You've gone a bit green. Feeling sick?"

"Mmm."

"You'll be fine when you get out of the car. Take a few deep breaths."

I breathed in and out, in and out, in and out. I felt so wobbly when I got out of the car that I had to lean against the door. I stared blearily at the house.

"Is *that* it?"

"Go on, Jane, be a sport. Dolphin came to u,
short notice. All my old faithfuls have got full h(

"I'm your oldest old faithful and my ,
couldn't be fuller . . . but there's always room for
more. Particularly one more Dolphin. Come in, ,
dear, and meet the family. You can skedaddle nov
Lizzie, she'll be fine with me."

So Lizzie went and I stayed.

"Right, Dolphin, here's my little babe," said Aunty
Jane, showing me into her bright yellow kitchen. A
rather yellowy baby with a very dribbly mouth was
strapped into a baby chair. It plucked at a string of
plastic rattles with its little primrose hands. Aunty Jane
tickled its fat tummy and it gurgled delightedly, drool-
ing all down its front.

"That's my little lovely," said Aunty Jane. "Come
and meet the rest of the family."

They were in the living room. There was a big television showing a Teletubbies video. Two Teletubbies
look-alikes were bumbling about in tiny T-shirts and
dungarees. The bigger one said a true Teletubby
Haro" to me and waved her chubby hand. The small
e sat down abruptly and blinked at me whilst it
ndered whether to start crying or not.

I wondered whether to cry too. I felt like Dorothy.
tepped into Oz.

Now, where are we going to put you?" said Aunty

It was a small terraced house with a postbox-red door and window frames, yellow curtains downstairs, blue upstairs. There was a green hedge and an untidy front garden with daisies and dandelions all over the long grass. It didn't look at all the sort of place the Foster Mother would live in. It looked like the sort of house I drew with my colored crayons.

Lizzie knocked at the scarlet front door. We heard cheery shouts and a wail or two and then the door opened and there was the Foster Mother. She was small and fat and old. She was also rather ugly, with gray hair cut in a schoolgirl clump and a very red face with a big nose that was almost purple. She had bright blue eyes, though, and a big smile. She smiled even more when she saw me.

"Who have we here? What's your name, sweet

"Dolphin."

"Dolphin? Ooh, I say, I've never met a Dolp fore. What a lovely name. I'm plain Jane. My n one look at me and decided anything fancy waste. You can call me Aunty Jane." Sh Lizzie. "Hello there, Busy Lizzie. Dolphir a big baby, isn't she?"

"I'm not a baby," I said.

"Precisely my point," said Aunty bies and toddlers. The under-fives remarkably big for your age, Dol bit over five to me."

Jane. "I don't think we can cram you into a crib! You'd better have Mark's room."

Mark was her youngest son, away at university. His room was still childish, with football and rock stars blue-tacked onto his walls and a faded Pamela Anderson poster above his bed.

"Not a girly room, I'm afraid," said Aunty Jane, puffing up the duvet, which was patterned all over with dinosaurs.

I suddenly felt so tired that all I wanted to do was crawl under that duvet and sleep but there was all sorts of other stuff I had to do first. I had to eat egg and chips for my tea and help Aunty Jane spoon runny boiled egg into two gaping toddler mouths and give the baby its bottle. I had to meet Uncle Eddie, who was old and gray like Aunty Jane. He called me Dolly Daydream. I had to have a bath and have my hair washed and my nails cut. I felt very scrubbed and scraped by the time Aunty Jane tucked me up into bed.

I went to sleep straightaway. But then I started dreaming. It was as if all the dinosaurs jumped straight off the duvet down my ear into my brain.

I had a beautiful sleek special dinosaur friend but she suddenly bounded away into the woods and I couldn't find her anymore. I was so lonely without her. I listened hard for her own special roar but I never heard it. So I made friends with some of the small dinosaurs. They were meek and friendly and grazed on grass and let me pet them but there were big ones too, huge and wild with great scaly tails and teeth that could tear me apart in one bite.

There was one with great glittering eyes and I thought at first it was gentle and grass-eating but when I tried to pet its long neck it snapped at me. I ran away from it, and then I got lost and I couldn't see where I was going. I was stumbling through this dark wood and I was so frightened.

I could hear the pounding of hard reptile feet running after me, the rasp of sharp claws and the thump of those terrible tails. They were getting nearer and nearer and then I was out of the forest but there was a vast black lake in front of me. I could see some creature swimming way out at the other side of the water. I wondered if I could reach it and whether it might tow me along. I knew I couldn't swim, but the fierce dinosaurs were there at my back, clawing at my dress, ripping it right off me, so I leapt into the lake. It was strangely warm and so wet, wet all over me. . . .

I woke up and realized what had happened. I lay there, sodden, my face screwed up with the shame. Then I got up, pulled the dripping sheet off the bed, bundled it up and crept to the bathroom. I ran cold water in the bath and steeped the sheet, wondering how I was ever going to get it dry. Then I heard footsteps.

"Dolphin? Dolphin, are you all right, sweetie? Are you just having a wee?"

I mumbled something and prayed she'd go away. She didn't. She waited outside the door a minute and then she said, "I'm coming in now, poppet."

She came in. She saw me in my wet nightie. She saw the sheet in the bath. She came over and hugged me.

"Never mind, little darling. It happens to the best of us. We'll pop you in the bath too—a *hot* one—and then we'll find you a nice clean nightie. It might have to be one of mine. It'll swamp you so you'll look a bit comic but never mind, eh?"

"You're not cross," I said.

"I'm not the littlest weeniest bit cross," she said.

When I was washed she wrapped me up in a big towel. She put the lid down on the lavatory and sat on it, with me on her lap, cuddled in close as if I were one of the babies.

I thought she'd let me off school the next morning but she said I should go.

"I'll take you, dear. It's all for the best. It'll take your mind off things."

"You don't know what it's like, Aunty Jane. It'll make everything much much worse."

"Nonsense."

"It's *sense*. I'm not going to school. And you can't make me."

She laughed. "Stop being such a saucy baggage!"

I sat down in her vast nightie and said I wasn't going to get washed or dressed.

She laughed again. "You'll look a right sight with me dragging you to school in that nightie! Still, it's raining, so we can spread it out, and all the babies can shelter underneath."

"That's silly."

"So are you. Now get washed and put on your dress. It's had a wash and all."

I nearly had another tantrum when I went to put on my poor witch frock. Its whirl in the washing machine had faded its bold black to dirty gray and it didn't have its own comforting smell anymore. All its remaining witchly powers had seeped away.

"It's come up a treat, your special frock," Aunty Jane said eagerly. "And look, I've found an old pair of Mark's socks—they'll be just the ticket."

They were long black socks. I found a pair of black Doc Martens at the back of his wardrobe. I tried them on. They looked incredible even if they were much too big. I wouldn't *need* witchly powers with big butch boots like them—one quick kick and old Ronnie Churley would go flying.

Aunty Jane fell about laughing when she saw what I'd put on.

"You can't wear them, sweetheart. They're a good six sizes too big for you."

"We could stuff them with socks."

"You've always got an answer for everything. Still, it makes a change from all my little kiddies. I like a good argument."

Aunty Jane won the argument too. I had to pad along to school in my own shabby sneakers. Uncle Eddie had to be off early in the car for his work so it was a problem getting all the babies ready and in the big buggy.

"I can go to school by myself, easy peasy," I said, but she wouldn't hear of it.

It was weird going to school from the other side of town. When we turned into the school road some of the kids started staring. Yvonne got out of her car at the school gates and looked at the babies openmouthed.

"Bye-bye, Dolphin. We'll come and collect you at twenty past three," said Aunty Jane, giving my dress a little tug straight.

"Who's she?" Yvonne demanded rudely.

"I'm Dolphin's Aunty Jane," said Aunty Jane. She gave me a quick kiss on the cheek and then set off homeward, clucking to the children.

"Are all them babies *hers*?" said Yvonne.

"Yes, she's a miracle of modern science," I said.

I pushed past her because I'd spotted Oliver in the playground. It was too far away for him to see me at first, but then he must have twigged that the black dot moving toward him was me. He started rushing toward me. It was like one of those silly romantic scenes in films. We even had our arms outstretched. But then we stopped at the last moment and stood still, grinning foolishly. We certainly weren't going to embrace in front of all the other kids in the school playground.

"Are you all right, Dolphin? I've been so worried! Where did you stay the night?"

"In a foster home. But it's OK," I said. "There are babies. Three of them."

"I like babies," said Oliver.

"Well, maybe you can come round and play with them. Aunty Jane won't mind."

"So she's an *aunty*?"

"Not a real one. But she's as good as."

"Oh, I'm so pleased! So can you stay with her?"

"I don't know. For a bit. Until . . . until my mum's better."

I didn't even want to say Marigold's name because that made it all too real and painful. I couldn't help thinking about her when lessons started. I kept seeing her lying in that bed drawing all over herself. I wanted to curl up round her and take her pen away and put my hands tight over hers to stop her hurting herself.

When it was playtime Miss Hill called me over to her desk.

"How are you today, Dolphin?" she said, her voice

all sweet and sticky as if she'd swallowed a tin of golden syrup.

I stared at her.

"You come and have a little chat with me if things are troubling you, dear."

Dear???

Mrs. Dunstan nodded at me in a weirdly matey way when she saw me in the corridor and I suddenly twigged. Lizzie must have phoned the school and told them what was going on, so now all the staff were being kind to the poor little kid who'd been taken into care.

I don't know if Mr. Harrison knew or not. He acted just the way he always did at lunchtime in the library. He gave Oliver and me a little wave when we walked in but didn't make a big deal of it. We sat together with our dolphin book. Mr. Harrison started rootling in his briefcase. We heard a promising rustle. He was unwrapping one of those wonderful giant bars of Cadbury's chocolate.

"It's magic munchie time!" he said, and he gave Oliver and me a third each.

School was certainly looking up. At this rate Ronnie Churley would blow kisses at me and Yvonne and Kayleigh would fashion me friendship bracelets and Tasha would beg me to stay over at her house and be her best friend forever.

Ronnie and Yvonne and Kayleigh and Tasha stayed their usual spiteful selves but the teachers were certainly trying hard. Especially Miss Hill.

It was story writing in the afternoon. Miss Hill said we had to pretend to be journalists. One of us would tell a story and the other would write it down. She told us to pair up.

Ronnie Churley groaned.

"It's not fair! I'm stuck with stupid old Dolphin who can't write for toffee."

"No, you're not," I said, and I darted across the room and bagged Oliver for my partner.

Miss Hill looked up . . . and said nothing at all! She let me stay with Oliver. So he got to be the reporter interviewing me. All the other kids pretended to be famous actors or football stars and just showed off about how much money they made. *I* decided to be the only survivor of a tragic accident at sea. I made out I was in hospital and talked about all my horrendous injuries, and how I felt so lonely and guilty being the only one on the ship left living. Oliver scribbled it all down, pages of it.

The reporters had to read out their interviews. Oliver got picked. Yvonne and Kayleigh started giggling at first when he started talking about this tragic shipwreck and everyone drowning but me, and how my lungs were so damaged I could barely whisper to tell him my dramatic true story but guess what! Miss Hill said it was excellent and gave us both a gold star!

It was the first time I'd ever been given a star for anything at school.

"That's just because she's being so creepy about you today," Kayleigh hissed. "What's up, Bottle Nose? Is it your mum? She hasn't died, has she?"

I suddenly saw Marigold flipped over on her back in bed in her strange white nightie, her hands clasped on her chest, her face a mask. I felt my eyes fill with tears.

"Oh, Kayleigh, that's an *awful* thing to say," said Yvonne. "Is it true, Dolphin?"

"I'm sorry, Dolphin. Don't cry," said Kayleigh.

They both looked anxiously at Miss Hill. If she saw I was crying they knew they'd be in for it.

I rubbed my eyes.

"She's not dead. But she's very ill. In hospital," I whispered.

They stared at me, their eyes round. Then Yvonne reached out. I thought she might be going to pinch me but she patted me on the shoulder instead.

"I hope she gets better soon," she said.

"Yes, so do I. I didn't mean what I said. I wasn't thinking," said Kayleigh.

It was great to have them desperate to make up to me but I couldn't get the image of Marigold dead out of my head.

I knew she'd tried to kill herself once when she was younger. She had two scars across her wrist. You could still feel them if you touched her, but you couldn't see them. She had twin tattoos covering them up, two horizontal lozenge-shaped diamonds with rays radiating out to show just how much they sparkled. She always said Star and I were her diamonds. But now Star had left her and I had put her in hospital.

I ran out of school the moment the bell went. I didn't even wait for Oliver. I thought I'd run right to the hospital but Aunty Jane was waiting for me at the gate with the baby buggy.

"Slow down, slow down, little Miss Speedy," she said. "Where are you off to? Not running away?"

"Not running away. Running *to* someplace. The hospital."

"Yes, poppet, you need to see your mum. Well, your dad's been in touch. He's coming to take you himself, after tea."

I was impressed by this but I argued all the same.

"I've got to see her now, Aunty Jane. You don't understand."

"I do, sweetheart, but the thing is, I can't let you skedaddle off to the hospital by yourself. I know you're a clever girl and could get there no problem at all, but I'm supposed to look after you and that means I'd have to tag along with you. How am I going to do that with a buggy full of babies who are going to start bawling for their tea any second now? Do you see my point?"

I had to see.

"Well, do you promise I can go to the hospital later? Even if my dad doesn't come for me?"

"If he doesn't come Uncle Eddie will take you. But your dad seems a man you can rely on."

Oliver came hurrying up then, a little wounded that I'd abandoned him but very eager to meet Aunty Jane and the babies. He didn't just treat them as babies either. He sorted out the difference between Celine and Martin and baby Daryl and shook each one by the small sticky fist. Martin was fussing by this time but became fascinated by Oliver's glasses and Daryl chuckled when Oliver gently tickled him under his damp chin.

"You're very good with the babies, darling," said Aunty Jane. "I think you'd better come home with us. You can keep them all amused while I put my feet up."

"Can Oliver really come, Aunty Jane? Can he come to tea?"

"Of course he can, so long as his mum doesn't mind."

"She will mind," said Oliver, sighing. "She got ever so upset about the other day. I'm in the doghouse at the moment."

He trotted off like a little spaniel, his long hair tufting in two clumps either side of his face like ears.

"He's a nice boy," said Aunty Jane. "Is he your special friend?"

"Yes, he is. Do you know what? I'm going to give him a haircut."

"Are you, dearie?"

I could tell by her tone she thought I was joking.

"I'm good at haircuts, really. I've got proper hair-dressing scissors. Well . . . back at home I have." My voice went a bit funny.

"He certainly could do with a good trim. He can barely see where he's going."

"I think he'd look great with it really really short. It would make him look much tougher."

"I think you'd better consult with his mum first," said Aunty Jane.

"Can I fetch my scissors then?"

"Yes, pet, when we've got a moment."

"I could give you a haircut too, if you like."

"What, a punk style?" said Aunty Jane.

We both cracked up laughing.

I went back to her house without any more argu-ments. The babies had milk and runny boiled egg and Marmite sandwiches for their tea. I started off with the same but I'd never had Marmite before. I ladled it onto my bread, mistaking it for chocolate spread. I practically choked to death at my first bite. Aunty Jane was sympa-thetic even though I spat my mouthful right out on my plate. She understood I couldn't fancy anything else sa-vory after that, so she made me two rounds of buttery toast spread with her own homemade strawberry jam. It was so good I golloped it down in no time. She made me two more slices, and then another two.

"You must think I'm the greediest girl in the whole world."

"I think it's great. You need feeding up, poppet, you're just a little scrap."

"My mum wasn't ever a great cook even when she was well," I said, slowing down a little.

"She probably had more important things on her mind," said Aunty Jane. "She sounds the artistic type. Your dad obviously thinks she's very special."

I chewed thoughtfully.

"She *is* special," I said. "She's just not all that great at doing mum things. Not like you."

"What is she great at, your mum?" said Aunty Jane.

I thought hard, still chewing.

"She's great at imagining stuff."

"Ah. Well, that's where I fall down. I can't imagine a bean. I could never make up a story to save my life."

"I can," I said.

"Then you take after your mum."

"Does that mean I'm going to go mad like my mum too?"

"You don't miss a trick, do you? Don't be too challenging, lovie, I'm used to dealing with babies. Well . . . I think your legs are planted too firmly on the ground for you to lose your head, if you get my drift."

I thought about my feet marching along the floor and wondered if my head could ever unscrew at the neck and spiral off on its own. I wondered if that was the way it felt to Marigold. She seemed to think everyone else was crazy, not her at all. I wondered how she was getting on in the hospital. She was so angry with me. Maybe it would only make her worse if I went to visit her?

I started chewing all round my fingernails.

"Don't eat your fingers, sugar lump," said Aunty Jane. "I can make more toast if you're still hungry."

"Do you think Michael really will come?"

"I'm sure he will."

"I'm not sure I want to go, though. Maybe my mum will be mean to me. She is sometimes." I tried to sound matter-of-fact but my voice wobbled.

"That's because she's ill, sweetheart. Maybe the hospital will make her better. Don't you fret about it. Don't think about the mean times just now. Come and have a cuddle."

"Do you know how mad I was?" I said indistinctly, my nose squashed up against Aunty Jane's big cushion chest. "I thought *you'd* be mean."

"Ooh, I can be," said Aunty Jane. She held me at arm's length and bared her teeth and growled until I got the giggles.

Michael was due to come at six o'clock. He came on the dot, right after *Neighbours*, just as Big Ben was chiming for the news on the telly.

"Here's your dad," said Aunty Jane.

"Hello," I said, feeling horribly shy.

He looked different. He was wearing a suit and his hair was neatly brushed. He looked a bit fierce at first but then I saw his eyes were still blinking a lot behind his glasses like a grown-up Oliver so I stopped feeling scared.

"Ready to visit your mum, Dolphin?" he said.

He sounded nervous too. We talked about her a bit on the way. He said he'd spoken to his doctor, who'd explained a lot about bipolar disorder.

"But of course she was just speaking in general terms. Marigold isn't an average sort of person. She's always been so different from anyone else."

"Did you love her?" I asked, glad that we were driving so he had to keep his eyes on the road.

"I loved her very much," said Michael.

"Do you still love her now?"

"Well. A lot of time's gone by. I love Meg now, and Grace and Alice. I've told them all about you and they can't wait to meet you."

"You wish," I said.

"No, it's true. Obviously, this has all been a bit sudden but we were wondering if you'd like to come this Sunday? If it's OK with your social worker and your foster mother? And you, of course?"

"Well . . ." I wondered if he *really* wanted me to come.

I peered at his profile. His eyes were blinking a lot. I

wondered if he'd ever love me. I wondered if I'd ever love him. It was weird thinking about it.

I forgot I hadn't given him an answer.

"I could take you swimming. But you don't have to come, not if you don't want to."

"I'm not sure about the swimming," I said. "But I'd like to come on Sunday. Please."

It turned out the trip to the hospital was a waste of time. Marigold had been very upset earlier and now she was "having a rest."

"They've tied her up in a straitjacket," I said, but when I peeped round her cubicle curtains she was lying freely in her bed, her eyes closed, her bright hair fanned out on the pillow. All the screaming ink people were scrubbed off her arms.

"She looks peaceful now anyway," said Michael, peeping too. "OK, we'll come back another time."

I leant over Marigold and gave her pale cheek a kiss.

"I love you," I whispered.

She stirred in her sleep and muttered something under her breath.

"No, it's not Star, it's Dolphin. Star loves you too," I said, though saying it made my mouth feel as if I were sucking lemons.

Michael didn't take me straight home. He took me to McDonald's and bought me a milk shake and an ice cream.

"Which flavor sauce do you like, Dolphin? Alice and

Grace are chocolate girls but I'm crazy about butterscotch."

"Me too!"

We smiled shyly at each other. It was quite hard finding enough to say when we were licking our ice creams. He started on about school stuff. I had to hedge a bit.

"So you're not too keen on school?"

"Is anyone?"

"Grace *loves* school. She can't wait to get there in the morning. Alice is a bit more reluctant. She's a bit of a chatterbox so she clowns around and gets told off. But she's very popular, even with the teachers."

"So they're clever, Alice and Grace?"

"Quite clever, yes."

"Star's clever. She's near the top of her class. Well, she was. But I'm not." I took a deep breath. "I'm not too great at reading, actually."

"You find stories a bit boring?"

"No, I like the stories. It's just the words. I can't read hard ones."

"Ah."

"I'm not thick. It's dyslexia. That's the proper word for it."

"Right. Well, I could try and help, if you like. I listen to Grace and Alice while they do their reading."

It looked as if it was going to be hard work hanging around with Michael. I didn't know which sounded worse, swimming lessons or reading sessions. But he didn't seem the sort of man who could get really cross. He seemed OK. Quite nice. He wasn't all hip and glamorous like Micky. But maybe I didn't want a dad like that.

Michael took me back to Aunty Jane's and said he'd come for me on Sunday. Then I helped Uncle Eddie bathe the babies while Aunty Jane made his supper, and then I was allowed to tuck each one up in its cot. I even got Daryl to sleep by plugging his mouth with a pacifier and rocking him. Then Aunty Jane and Uncle Eddie and I had chicken and chips on trays in front of the television.

Aunty Jane made wonderful chips. She gave me a huge plateful. I was just daring to feel happy when the doorbell rang.

"Drat," said Aunty Jane. "Who is it at this time?"

My tummy went tight. I put my knife and fork down. I wondered what had happened. I started biting my fingers.

I heard Aunty Jane and Lizzie out in the hall. Aunty Jane called me.

"You'll never guess who's here, Dolphin!"

Star was standing in the hall. She looked prettier than ever, her lovely blond hair braided into little plaits tied with beads and colored threads—and she had a diamond stud sparkling in her nose.

THE FULL PICTURE

We ran to each other and hugged as hard as we could. Aunty Jane smiled and Uncle Eddie went all watery-eyed and had to blow his nose. Lizzie leapt in quick and asked if they'd mind having Star too, just for a few days, until everything could be properly sorted out for both of us.

So Star and I ended up sharing Mark's bed. I cried a bit and she did too and then we went to sleep curled up together. I breathed in her sweet powdery smell and wound one of her silky plaits round my finger and she cuddled in to me and held on to me so tightly she made little bruises on my arms, real fingermarks.

It was different in the morning when all the explanations started. Star woke me up by giving me a thump on the shoulder.

"*Why* wouldn't you switch the new phone on?" she said. "I was so worried about you. I was scared something had happened. It was so mean of you to smash the first phone and then tell all those lies and then not even *use* the new phone. I didn't know what had happened. I felt I was going to go crazy worrying. I even got Micky to send *another* phone just in case the last one got lost in the post. He kept telling me that you and Marigold were just mad at me and deliberately trying to make me worry and that I should just stay cool and enjoy my time with him but I couldn't. It all got spoilt, Micky and me. That's what you wanted, wasn't it? You couldn't let me have a bit of happiness just for myself."

"I can't believe you're saying all this rubbish," I said. I thumped her back. "Don't you dare get angry with me! *You're* the one who walked out on me and left me with Marigold at her absolute worst. You didn't care. She really went crazy, she practically beat me up. It's *true*. Then she painted herself all over and I was so scared that I had to call an ambulance. Why should I answer your stupid phone when you won't listen to me or come back to help me and you won't even give me Micky's stupid number? *I* didn't muck up your time with him. Look, I don't need you anymore. I've got my own life, a whole new life just for me. What makes you think you've got the right to barge in here? This is *my* foster home, not yours. I had to get it all sorted out because you left me. When Marigold went into hospital I didn't have anyone. *You* didn't care, just so long as you could stay with your precious Micky."

"I did care. I got so that I couldn't even think straight. I started to act stupid. Micky was very sweet about it, ever so understanding, but that Sîan started saying stuff, forever getting at me. I don't know what Micky sees in her. She just hung around all the time, she'd never leave us on our own. We ended up having this huge row. It was all too much hassle for Micky. He said he'd drive me all the way home just so as I could check up on you. Then you weren't there, Marigold wasn't there. I just about went crazy. Mrs. Luft told me Marigold had been taken to hospital and she said you'd gone off with your dad. That was the worst thing ever because you haven't *got* a dad."

"I have too. I've got my *own* dad. I found him all by myself. Well, with Oliver. He's great, my dad. He keeps coming to see me. He's invited me round to his place on Sunday. He takes me to see Marigold in the hospital."

"How could you have sent her to the hospital? You know how she feels about them. Why couldn't you have looked after her just for a bit till I came back?"

"I didn't think you were *ever* coming back. I had to do something. She'd covered herself all over with paint and then she just stood there and she wouldn't talk to

275

me or anything. She went really really mad and I didn't know what else to do."

"You said she went mad before but you were just making it up to get me to come back."

"Are you saying I'm a liar?"

"Yes. Liar liar liar!"

I got hold of a fistful of her little plaits and yanked them hard. She jerked herself free and kicked me so that I nearly tumbled out of bed. I clenched my fists and tried to hit her.

"Mind my diamond!" she shrieked.

"You think it looks so cool but it looks *stupid*."

"Well, you *always* look stupid. I'm so sick of being stuck with you."

"So clear off, why don't you? Rush back to your precious Micky. I don't need you anymore."

"Right. I will. Today. Fine," Star declared, but she didn't sound convincing.

"He doesn't want you anymore, does he?"

"Yes he does! Of course he does. It's just . . ."

"He's got fed up with you just the way he got fed up with Marigold."

"No, stop it. Shut up, you hateful little cow. He *does* want me. He's coming back for me. You'll see. Don't you dare say he won't."

She slapped me right across the face. I slapped her back, knocking her sore nose. Then we were really fighting, rolling over and over until we both fell off the bed and then hitting and kicking as we struggled on the carpet.

"Girls! Girls! For heaven's sake, look at the pair of you. Stop it this instant!" Aunty Jane was standing in the doorway in her vast quilted dressing gown.

We stopped, puffing and panting, scarlet with rage.

"Dear goodness, are you the same sisters who fell asleep in each other's arms like the Babes in the Wood?" said Aunty Jane, sitting down on the floor between us. She tried to put her arms round both of us. I was glad when Star flinched away, tossing her plaits. She was *my* Aunty Jane and I didn't want to share her.

"She started it," I said. "She woke me up by hitting me."

"Now now, don't tell tales," said Aunty Jane.

I burst into tears, not able to stand it that she was telling me off.

"Hey, poor little snugglepuss," said Aunty Jane, cuddling me close. "No need for tears, poppet."

"God, do you have to act like a baby?" Star said. She checked her nose gingerly and tidied her plaits.

"I'm used to babies," said Aunty Jane, rocking me. "She's just doing it to be obliging, Star. You sure you don't want to make this old lady's day by joining in the cuddle?"

"No, thanks. I don't want to play silly games," said Star.

"That's rich coming from you, when you kept putting

on that dopey little girl act for Micky. Only now he's dumped you on the social services, hasn't he?" I said.

"I told you, quit it!" Star threatened.

"Why don't we all quit it," said Aunty Jane.

One of the babies started crying.

"Oh dear. It sounds like waking up for breakfast time. I'd better go and see to him. Will you two girls promise not to murder each other during the next half hour?"

We glared at each other and then burst out laughing. Aunty Jane shook her head at us and went off, baby-bound. We giggled hysterically though it really wasn't funny.

"We're mad," said Star.

"Are we going to end up like Marigold? Star, I *had* to get her into hospital."

"I would have done the same. I'm sorry I wasn't there. I just so badly had to be with Micky."

"I know."

"He hasn't dumped me, though. I mean, we had to get in touch with the social services, but it was because we were looking for *you*. But then they sort of took over. Micky will be back for me, you'll see. I mean, there are problems. Like Sîan. But Micky told me privately that I'm far more important to him than she is. He says he's going to get rid of her soon anyway."

I kept nodding until she'd finished.

"I like your hair," I said.

"Someone in the street did hair wrapping and they plaited all of mine."

"Let's see how it's done." I examined a plait carefully. "Aha. *I* see. Yeah," I said, working it out.

"Could you do them like this for me again sometime?"

"I think so."

"Do you really think my diamond looks stupid?"

"No. It looks great."

"It's a *real* diamond. Micky did it for me. It hurt but I didn't cry. You really think it looks cool?"

"Yes, I love it. Tell you one thing, though. Marigold will go crazy when she sees it."

"Marigold *is* crazy," said Star.

We started giggling again, guiltily.

"Is she really bad?" Star asked.

"She's the worst ever."

But when Uncle Eddie drove us both to the hospital that evening Marigold was different. She wasn't in bed. She was sitting up in a chair doing some sort of sewing, wearing a hospital stripy toweling dressing gown. The orange and green and black made her tattoos look especially garish. She was slumped, her hair badly needing a wash, but when she saw us coming she sat up straight.

Uncle Eddie went to have a cup of coffee while we walked up the squeaky polished floor to our mother.

"Thank God! Where have you been, you two?" Then she remembered. "Is Micky with you, Star?" Her voice was strange, slurred. I wondered if she'd managed to stow some vodka away.

Star shook her head. "He's gone back to Brighton."

"Oh." She slumped again, throwing down the sewing. "So what was that other Micky doing here? How many other boyfriends are going to come crawling out of the woodwork? And I look such a mess too." She picked up her toweling belt and chucked it back in her lap in disgust. "This is so hideous. I want my own stuff."

"OK. I'll bring it for you tomorrow," said Star.

"Can't you get me out of here? It's sheer bloody torture," said Marigold. "They're trying to poison me."

"What's that you're saying, darling?" said a cheery nurse tending an old lady in the next bed.

"You're *poisoning* me," said Marigold. "Look, girls, look." She held out her hands. They were shaking quite badly. "I've got the shakes and my voice sounds weird, all thick and old and horrible, and I keep throwing up. I tell you, they're poisoning me."

"It's your reaction to lithium, sweetheart," said the nurse.

"Yes, you're giving me poisonous drugs."

"It's a natural salt, and it'll work wonders if you let it. Take your lithium like a lamb every day and you'll soon be back home with your girls," said the nurse. "That's what you want, isn't it?"

Marigold opened her eyes wide as if she was seeing properly for the first time.

"That's what I want," she said. Her eyes filled with huge tears. "That's what I want. My girls," she said, and she held out her arms.

We went to her and she held us close, one either side, her hands hanging on to the folds of our clothes.

"I'm sorry," she whispered.

"I'm sorry I went away and left you," Star said.

"I'm sorry I called the ambulance," I said.

"No, *I'm* sorry. I'm the useless hateful bad mother," Marigold wept. "I had to do this stupid talking thing today. It's supposed to make me feel better and stop me drinking. It didn't make me feel better, I felt much *worse*. I was sick, but they still wouldn't let me go back to bed. They went on and on asking me stuff about when I was little, so in the end I blurted out all sorts of ugly things about my mother and all she'd done to me and how I hated her. Then I realized, I'm the same. I've done some of the same stuff to you two. You must both hate me."

"We don't hate you, we love you, you silly woman," said Star, hugging her.

"We love you to bits," I said, and then I pricked myself on her sewing. "Ouch. What's this?"

There were odd little squares and rounds and diamonds of all different-colored material.

"It's occupational bloody boring therapy," said Marigold. "This awful woman has started me off making a quilt, just because I said I liked sewing. It's not my scene at all, quilts!"

"But the pieces don't fit together properly," I said.

"Aha," said Marigold. "Guess what kind of quilt this is going to be. Would you believe it's called a crazy quilt?"

Star snorted with laughter and had to blow her nose. Marigold looked at her and then looked again.

She screamed.

"Dear God, what is it now?" said the nurse, running over.

"Look! She's had her beautiful little nose pierced! Star, how *could* you? What does it look like!"

She carried on as if she were the most uncool conventional mum in the world, with virgin skin. I looked at her, my illustrated mum. I knew she really did love me and Star. We had a father each and maybe they'd be around for us and maybe they wouldn't—but we'd always have our mum, Marigold. It didn't matter if she was mad or bad. She belonged to us and we belonged to her. The three of us. Marigold and Star and Dolphin.

About the Author

Jacqueline Wilson has written more than seventy award-winning books for young readers of all ages. She lives near London in a small house crammed with fifteen thousand books. Her previous Delacorte Press books include *The Suitcase Kid, Double Act, The Lottie Project, Bad Girls, The Story of Tracy Beaker, Vicky Angel, The Worry Web Site* and the GIRLS Quartet.